IN TOO DEEP

E.R. Hendricks

ISBN-13: 9798780982616
ISBN-10: 1477123456

Cover design by: E.R. Hendricks
Library of Congress Control Number: 2018675309
Printed in the United States of America

This book is dedicated To all my readers, thank you so much for your support and know I love you all!

CONTENTS

BLURB

The Mountain has always been my safe place, until it wasn't.

It was the place I went to escape from my mundane 9-5 desk job. My secret spot that allowed me to finally take a deep breath and clear my head.

It's where I escaped the darkness that always follows me.

I never thought it would all come crashing down around me.

Trapped with nowhere to go, I am forced to depend on the one man I promised myself I would never even speak to again, none-the-less depend on.

In too Deep is a novella with enemies to lovers, forced proximity, CEO/boss, age gap tropes. This book has a HEA. It is recommended for 18+ due to language, sexual situations and violence. If you like spice this book is for you. Happy reading.

TRIGGER WARNING

CHAPTER 1

Aleice

Fuck, today sucked. I rub my forehead with my hand before resting it on the bar top.

"What'll it be?" the bartender asks me with a small smirk on his face.

"Vodka cran, please."

He nods and gets to work, making my drink. I glance around the dingy bar, noticing the heavy feeling of eyes that usually follow me is noticeable absent. There aren't many people here because Ron's is more of a dive bar than anything. It's actually one thing I like most about it—that and the cheap drinks.

He hands me my drink and I hand him my card. "Keep my tab open." His eyes connect with mine and I can see the mirth in his. Well, I'm glad my shitty day amuses someone.

I'm about four sips in when someone plops down in the seat next to me. I glance over and see what honestly could be a white whale. And I don't mean because of his slightly graying hair; I mean because this man is beyond *gorgeous.* Men don't look like this anymore. I take in his strong stubbled jaw from the side. He has long eyelashes that fan out over his defined cheekbones. His hair is just long enough to run your fingers through, like an outgrown military cut. His broad shoulders almost reach me from his stool. He's wearing a white dress shirt that hugs his shoulders and arms like a glove. He's rolled up the sleeves, giving me a perfect view of his toned forearms. I quickly glance away before he catches me ogling him.

"Crown on the rocks, Ron," he says to the bartender before he even has time to walk over to him. Ron nods his head and gets to work.

Even his voice is sexy, and he smells good. Fuck, I need to settle down. I take a deep breath, trying to relax with this sexy silver fox next to me. Shit, that was a bad idea. All I ended up doing was breathing in his cologne further. I take a few more sips of my drink before Ron hands over his drink.

I continue to look around the bar, trying very hard not to stare at the mirror behind the bar so I can see what Mr. Sexy is doing.

"Long day?" I hear in a smooth deep tone, the sound vibrates through me. I whip my head around to him before my brain even processes that the words he spoke were directed at me.

"Yeah, just working on an enormous project." I shake my head, showing I really don't want to talk about it. He nods his head in understanding.

"What about you?" I ask, trying to keep the conversation going.

"Something similar, actually," he smirks, and I see as his eyes drop as he takes me in.

This is where I wish I could be witty and confident, but honestly, I'm a computer geek who spends most of her time behind a monitor, around dudes who wear pocket protectors. I'm saved from my awkwardness when he continues the conversation.

"Let's not talk about work, let's just keep it simple." He offers his hand for me to shake. "My name's Shaw, it's nice to meet you…"

"Aleice, and it's nice meeting you too, Shaw," I smile as I take his hand. Small tingles race down my arm to my shoulder. My smile slips slightly and my brows furrow. That was weird. I glance at him to see if he felt it too, but he's just looking at me. Probably just static electricity.

As the night went on, we both let loose a little, laughing and joking, and flirting. "How long have you lived in New York?" He asks as I sip my drink. "I've lived here my whole life. I don't know what I would do without traffic." I laugh at my own joke and he chuckles into his glass. My eyes rake over his lips, now wet with Crown. *God, I want to lick it off.* Shaking that thought away, he places his hand on my thigh, rubbing his thumb back and forth over my jeans. I could feel the sexual tension vibrating through my body. "You?" I use my finger to slide my glasses back up my nose. "Yep, except for my time spent serving," he says, and we laugh while he tells stories of his adventures while overseas. This guy is something else. He's smart, confident, sexy, and funny and I don't want this night to end.

"I'm sorry, you two, but it's last call," Ron says as he finishes cleaning the glasses and wiping down the bar top. I didn't want this night to end. I haven't laughed this much in such a long time and haven't felt this carefree and alone.

He spins on his stool until he is facing me. "Come home with me," he says, his voice confident and not even a little slurred. My eyes widen in shock. This Adonis wants to sleep with me? Am I stupid to turn it down, or stupid to take him up on his offer?

I nod my head and smile. The alcohol gives me the confidence to agree without the over-whelming sense of dread I usually get when men ask this of me. I almost always turn them down, but every once in a while, I'd agree—hey, a girl's got needs too. The guys I usually attract—or maybe it's because I'm a female working in a predominantly male field—tend to be nerds and computer geeks, and not the sexy kind you see in movies.

I grab my jacket as we head outside.

"I ordered us an Uber. Should be here any minute."

I glance over at my car, one of the few left in the parking lot.

"We can take an Uber back in the morning and grab the cars." He smiles.

Feeling a little better, I get into the back of the Uber and pull out my phone, discreetly send-ing a text to my best friend and roommate Jamie, letting her know I have my location on and I'm out for the night. I put my phone away and push my glasses back up my nose. He chuckles and shakes his head.

"What?" I ask, a smile on my face too.

"Nothing, you just have this whole sexy nerd vibe going on." A cocky smirk lay on his beautiful face. His eyelids lower as he takes me in again before licking his full lips.

I bite mine, wishing I had the guts to lean forward and kiss him. As if reading my mind, he does just that. As his lips touch mine, his right hand comes around and entangles in my hair, fisting it at my nape and controlling the kiss. He slides his tongue over my bottom lip before moving to my top one. I moan at the sensation, and he uses the opportunity to slide his tongue inside my mouth. This kiss is amazing. It's demanding and soft all at once. It's powerful but controlled. He uses his hand to turn my head and deepen the kiss as his tongue continues to caress mine.

We break apart at the sound of a throat clearing. "You're here."

I blush at the thought of the driver seeing us kissing. Shaw smirks again before he kisses me one more time, gets out, and comes around the car to open my door. He grabs my hand and helps me out.

"Thank you," I say as I take his hand.

He keeps my hand in his as he leads me into a fancy apartment building. We are still in the city and not too far from the office. That's good. Worse comes to worst, I can just walk to work in the morning. He leads me through the front door and over to the elevator where he scans a keycard. "Security," he tells me by way of explanation. I just smile and nod. Not any of my business.

As we reach the top floor, the doors open right into the penthouse. My eyes must be as wide as saucers as I take in the opulence in this apartment. Floor-to-ceiling windows give a full view of the New York skyline. It's modern with hints of industrial, exposed duct work and masculine accents. As I walk further in, I see it's all open-concept with a vast fireplace to the left and a large kitchen on the right separated by a spacious island with white granite waterfall sides, against matte black cabinets. He has two leather club chairs in front of the fireplace and a luxurious gray couch that looks comfortable enough to sleep on. He watches me as I take it all in, and he chuckles.

"It's beautiful," is all I can think to say as I continue to look at the high ceilings and the professional grade appliances.

"Thank you." He grabs my hand and pulls me down a hallway to the right, past the kitchen. We pass about four more doors before we end up at the end of the hallway and to a set of double doors. As he pulls me inside, I can't help but gasp. His Cali king-sized bed is straight ahead against an exposed brick wall. The rest of the walls are a charcoal gray color. He has long corded Edison bulbs hanging over his nightstands and his bed looks comfortable enough to live in.

CHAPTER 2

Shaw

I watch as she takes in my apartment. God, she is beautiful, with her mousy brown hair and her blue eyes that pop behind her big round framed glasses. She has a cute little nose and pouty, soft lips. My eyes work their way down her body as I take in her generous bust and slim waist before I get to a small but perky round butt in her fitted jeans. She's not my typical type, but there is just something about her. She's so authentic. I really enjoy that about her. She almost seems a little shy, and it's fucking adorable. I watch as she uses her finger to push her glasses up her face again from where they have slipped down her pert little nose.

I unbutton my shirt as she continues to take everything in. By the time she turns around, my shirt is slipping off my shoulders and her eyes widen, her pupils dilate as she takes in my muscular form. I may be getting up there in age, but I pride myself on going to the gym and staying in good shape. I'd be a shitty bodyguard if I couldn't protect my clients and run down an assailant. I see a blush go to her cheeks and I smirk as I admire her.

She bites her lip and takes a step closer to me before reaching out and running her hands over my shoulders and down my chest and abs. She lets out a small groan that I'm not even sure she's aware she made. I chuckle softly, which seems to snap her out of her daze as she shakes her head and blushes a shade of red I've only seen on a tomato.

"It's okay baby, you can enjoy my body," I tell her as I take her hands and put them back on me. She lets out a little sigh. I slowly run my fingertips down her arms, and she shivers. I continue over her shoulders and down her slender curves before reaching the hem of her t-shirt. "May I?" She nods her head enthusiastically and I pull her shirt over her head. I take a step back to admire her large, full breasts as they threaten to spill from her cups with each deep inhalation.

I watch as her blush makes its way down her neck and across her chest. I growl at the sight and wrap my hands around both breasts before squeezing them firmly. Sliding my hand around her back and popping open the clasp of her bra, I expose her breasts.

"Fuck," she moans, as my thumbs rub gently over each small, stiff pink nipple.

"Fuckin' A, you have the most beautiful tits I've ever seen," I groan as I lower my mouth to suck on her right nipple. She moans as I flick my tongue back and forth before nibbling my way over to her other breast. I lick and suck and nip all over her breasts and nipples. Not being able to stand it any longer, I throw her over my shoulder and she yelps in surprise. I take the six steps over to my bed and lay her down on her back before kissing my way down her flat stomach to the waistband of her jeans. I look up and wait. Understanding my unspoken question, she nods her head eagerly. I smirk and unbutton her jeans and slowly work them down her legs, teasing us both. Fuck, she has nice legs.

I groan as I see her lying across my bed in just a black lace thong that barely covers her tiny pussy. I lick my lips as I imagine what her delicious little cunt will taste like. She bites her lip, and I can tell she's slowly losing her shyness as her desire builds. I take my time kissing my way up her calf towards her thigh before passing over her center and working my way down her other thigh. She groans and lifts her hips to try to encourage me where she wants me. I smile against her leg and continue my descent, teasing with little bites as I go.

"Please..." she begs as the wet spot on her panties grows larger. I take my time, working my way back up her thigh, then run my nose up her slit over her panties, taking a deep breath and breathing in her sweetness. Unable to resist, I lick the outside of her panties to taste her wetness. She moans and I almost give in and just take her, but I want to enjoy this a while longer. I slide my fingers under the waistband and slide her panties down her luscious legs before tossing them aside. It's then I see her pretty pink slit for the first time, and I can't help but moan as I palm my now hard-as-steel cock over my pants. She moans as she watches me and reaches for my belt. I let her, if only for the slight relief I will get from freeing my stiffness from the confines of my dress pants. She gets it undone and I slide them and my boxers down together.

"Oh God!" she says as she takes in the first sight of my cock that's now on full display, pointing directly at her. I know I am much larger than your average man, so I give her a second in case she wants to back out.

She tentatively reaches out, and then grabs ahold of me firmly. She strokes me once, twice, slowly but firmly from root to tip, "I...I'm not sure it'll fit," she whispers, almost to her herself.

I can't help the smug smile that crosses my face. "Don't worry baby, I'll get you nice and wet before we try anything." With that said, I lower myself back down her body until I'm level with her perfect pussy. She takes a deep breath as she pants with anticipation. I hover above her slowly, breathing out hot air over her wet center before she begs again and thrusts up to meet my face. I give in and, while her hips are up, slide my hands under her ass so I can wrap my hands over her hips and hold her thighs in place. My first lick is from her opening to her clit. I growl at the taste of her. So fucking good; sweet with a hint of something that's entirely her. She moans as she grabs my hair and holds my face to her slit. I work my tongue around her swollen nub as I feel her cream drenching my chin. Fuck, she's so wet for me. I suck her bud into my mouth and pulse until she's losing it and she screams my name as she orgasms. I let go and gently swirl my tongue around her clit again to prolong her pleasure. Once her body relaxes, I release her hip with my right hand. I slide it out from underneath her to insert two fingers into her tight pussy, working them in and out. My mouth continues its assault, slowly building her to another climax.

"You taste so good, baby girl," I murmur into her soft folds as I nip and lick her pussy.

"That feels so good, don't stop," she pants out.

I feel her walls start to tighten around my fingers and I know she's close. I feel along the top of her channel until I feel her g-spot, then rub my finger over the area, applying pressure until her moans get louder and louder. I feel the moment she comes as she squirts all over my face, and screams so loud, I'm pretty sure the people on the eighth floor can hear her. I smile with male satisfaction that I did that.

"Oh my God, I don't think I've ever come that hard before," she says as she comes back down from her high.

My cock is so hard I'm pretty sure I'm punching a hole in the bed. "You're so beautiful when you come," I say as I look her in the eyes and swipe my thumb across my chin before sucking it into my mouth, cleaning off all her cream.

She grabs me by my arms, trying to pull me up on top of her. I oblige as I kiss her mouth, hard and rough, making her taste herself on my tongue. She moans and kisses me back just as hard.

She pulls back. "Fuck me, please," she begs as she reaches down for my engorged cock and tries to bring it to her entrance. I stop her and reach over to the nightstand and grab a condom before tearing open the wrapper. She nods her head, silently thanking me for being responsible. I just smirk and slide the condom down my fat shaft. I grab myself at the base and guide it back to her opening before sliding my head in. It's a very tight fit, but I continue to slowly work myself inside her.

"Fuck yes, daddy!" She exclaims, and then freezes. Her eyes get huge and her hand flies to her mouth like she can't believe she just said that. Normally that's not my kind of kink, but if I'm being honest, I don't mind it coming from her. She's got this innocence that makes it seem genuine instead of when girls fake it to be sexy.

"I can be your daddy," I tell her as I bottom out in her tight little cunt. I still for a moment, letting her adjust as I lean forward with my elbows by her head and lick my way from her collarbone all the way up to just under her ear. She moans and her nails drag down my back. When she starts to rock her pelvis against me, I slowly back out before thrusting hard back in. I repeat this motion for a while until she whimpers and whines at my pace.

"Please, daddy…" she moans, begging, and I almost nut right then and there.

She wants a daddy. Oh, I'll be her daddy. I pull out and quickly flip her over before lifting her hips with my hands. I line myself back up and slam myself back into her.

"Oh, God… yes!" she screams. Holding her hips in my hands, I thrust into her harder and faster. Testing the waters, I smack her ass once, just enough to sting. She yelps in shock, but quickly moans and pushes back against me.

Ah, my little nerd likes it rough. I rear back and give her ass a few more slaps, making it nice and red. I can tell she's really getting into it; her cream is dripping down my balls and I don't think I've ever been this fucking hard. In fact, I don't think sex has ever been this fucking good.

"Shaw, Shaw, yesss…" she hisses out, and I feel her pussy clamp down like a vice around my cock and I can't hold back anymore. I pull her body up against mine so her back is to my front, and I pound into her from underneath. I pluck and pinch her nipples, already building her back up.

"You like that, don't you, dirty girl?" I whisper in her ear as my right hand snakes up to wrap around her throat, just tight enough to let her know I'm in control.

"God, yes!" she moans, barely coherent in her pleasure.

Fuck, it feels so good, but I want her fat, juicy tits in my face. I easily lift her, turning her around so she's facing me now to ride my cock. As she slides back down, she throws her head back and starts to bounce up and down on my lap. "Fuck, you're so sexy baby girl." I grab her left breast and lift it to my mouth so I can flick my tongue back and forth over her nipple. I work the other one with my thumb and forefinger. Her nipples seem to be really sensitive. I love how responsive she is to me. She brings her head back and her eyes lock on mine. And suddenly this seems like more than just sex. I mean it's really good fucking sex, but I've never connected with a woman like this before. It's always just been sex, good till it's over. She runs her hands over the sides of my face until they slide into my hair, her nails gliding against my scalp.

"You feel so good inside me," she says as she lightly tugs my hair, bringing my face to hers to kiss me. Her lips slide against mine with so much passion it's hard to focus. I grab her hips and help guide her as she continues to work herself on me. I bounce her harder as I thrust faster up into her.

"That's it baby, ride my cock," I groan

"Oh, God... Shaw," she whimpers as she throws her head back and finishes one last time for me, her pussy clamping down on me so tight it triggers my orgasm. I roar her name as I finish deep inside her. Her head rests on my shoulder as we catch our breath and come down from our highs.

"Fuck, baby. That was amazing." No sense in denying it, we've got amazing chemistry, and that translated to amazing sex.

Lifting her up, I carry her to the bathroom while my cock is still inside her. I plant her ass on the countertop and pull myself out of her perfect pussy, now swollen with use. I pull the condom off and toss it into the trash before I turn on the shower.

"Want to hop in?" I ask, tossing my thumb over my shoulder to indicate the shower.

"Yes, please." She slides off the counter and joins me in the shower. She's back to blushing now that we are done.

"I'm sorry I called you daddy... I have no clue where that came from." She bows her head in her hands in embarrassment.

I chuckle and remove her hands. "There is nothing to be sorry for, darlin'. I actually enjoyed it. I'll admit, I didn't think I would, but with you, it was sexy." I tell her honestly, not just to temper her embarrassment. I wash her down, enjoying the act of touching her beautiful body, even if it isn't sexual.

Once we are both clean, I throw her one of my undershirts, and try not to laugh when it looks like a dress. She giggles when she sees herself in the mirror. It hangs down almost to her knees.

I'm already in a fresh pair of boxers and

under the covers. I pat the spot next to me. She smiles and climbs in beside me. I grab her waist and pull her into my side. She snuggles in with her head on my chest and makes a cute little content noise. I smile and kiss her head, saying, "Goodnight sweetheart."

"Night." She throws her leg over me and after taking a few deep breaths, I hear her breathing level out.

I tilt my head back to look down at her as she softly snores. God, this girl is fucking adorable. I kiss her head again, enjoying the feel of her in my arms. It's been a long time since I just... was. I'm always Shaw the CEO, Shaw the boss, Shaw the Marine, it's nice to sit back and spend time with someone who has no clue who I am, I'm just a guy she's interested in, and she wants nothing from me but sex. It's refreshing. I relax and let myself drift off to sleep.

CHAPTER 3

Aleice

I wake up early, thank God, because I'm not sure I can face Shaw in the light of day. I slowly slide away from him and sneak out of bed, trying to be as quiet as possible, grabbing my glasses off the nightstand.

I'm awful at one-night stands. I get too attached and I know that's not what Shaw is interested in. Grabbing all of my clothes off the floor, I slowly make my way out into the hallway, closing the door behind me. Once I'm out in the open floor plan living and kitchen area, I dress quickly. Feeling guilty about leaving early, even if it's most likely what he wants, I find his coffee and make him a pot and set it to stay warm. Hopefully, it's still warm by the time he wakes up. I also find a pad of sticky notes and a pen and say that I had to get to work early and leave my number on the rare chance that he wants to get together again.

Grabbing my shoes, I head to the elevator. Once the doors close, I put my shoes on. I take a deep breath and prepare for the walk of shame. At the ground floor, I bow my head as I make my way through the lobby, making sure not to make eye contact with the doorman. God, this is so embarrassing. It's not that I'm ashamed of sex—not in the slightest. It's just that everyone knows exactly what we did. My hair looks like a small bird has nested in it and I'm sure we smeared my makeup across my face, yeahhh... I'm not exactly making any fashion statements this morning. Self-consciously running my hands through my hair, I open the Uber app and I see one is only two minutes away.

"Thank the heavens someone is on my side," I mutter. About three minutes later, the driver pulls up and I have her take me back to the bar to retrieve my car.

"Thank you," I murmur as I get out of the Uber and head to my car. Once safely inside, I slump in the seat and allow myself to think about last night. That was the most amazing sex I've ever had. I can still feel the pleasant ache of him between my legs. That cock... it was like a baby's arm. I giggle to myself. The way he used it, though, he was so confident and took control over it all. It was not something I am used to. I didn't know how much I longed for that. How much I needed a man instead of the boys I've been hooking up with. I roll my eyes as I turn the car over and crank the heat. It's so cold in New York in December; I love living in the city, but it definitely has its downsides.

Once I'm at my apartment building, I pull into my designated parking spot and walk up to the third floor. It's not in the best part of the city and it's not the best apartment and I still need a roommate in order to afford it—one of said downsides. I unlock the door and take my shoes off so I don't wake my roommate Jamie.

It's then that a light flicks on in the corner over one of are armchairs, where Jamie is currently sitting. She has her arms crossed over her chest.

"You want to tell me where you've been all night?" she huffs out and I chuckle.

"Oh, I'm sorry mom, did I not send you a text with my location?" I sass.

"Oh, smartass, you did, but that doesn't mean he wasn't a serial killer and didn't kill you right after you sent it."

I roll my eyes. "Wow, okay, CSI. Thanks for cracking the case." I walk toward my room since I have to get ready for work. As I pass the kitchen, I flick on the coffee maker.

"I'm serious Aleice, I was worried about you."

I stop and turn around to see her following behind me. "I'm sorry. I didn't mean for you to worry." I smirk and bite my lip.

She smirks then, too. "Good, was it?" She chuckles.

"Girl, you have no idea!" I groan as I turn to head back to my room.

I quickly take off my old clothes and toss them into the hamper in the corner. After taking a quick pee and brushing my teeth, I come back out and go through my dresser to find a clean pair of jeans and a fresh t-shirt. I throw on a hoodie and head back out to the kitchen to fix myself a cup of coffee. Just the way I like it—black with a splash of creamer, I stir it before taking a healthy sip.

"Ahh, the nectar of the gods," I moan.

Jamie giggles as she gets herself a cup. "So, are you going to give me any more information, or am I going to have to just use my imagination?" she wiggles her eyebrows at me.

I purse my lips to the side and squint one eye in dramatic thought. "It was the best sex I've ever had… and I may have accidentally called him daddy," I groan and she spits her coffee out of her mouth, pitching over in a fit of laughter.

"How does that just slip out?" she laughs.

I face palm. "I have no clue!" I exaggeratedly whisper at her.

She continues to laugh. When she finally comes up for air, she looks at me and says, "What did he say to that?"

I bite my lip. "He said he could be my daddy." My eyes slide to the right as I say it.

"Holy shit! That's hot." She bites her lip and fans her face dramatically.

I bite my lip and nod.

"So, are you going to see daddy again?" She giggles.

I blow out a puff of air. "Probably not. I was under the impression it was just a one-night stand and I highly doubt someone that gorgeous would want any more than that with me."

Her shoulders drop. "You're a great catch Aleice, you're the complete package—funny, smart, and beautiful."

I blush. "Thanks," I mumble, never knowing how to take a compliment.

I finish my coffee and put my mug in the sink. I still have an hour before work, but I have some stuff I want to get caught up on with the extensive project I'm working on, so I figure I'll just head in early and take care of it.

"See you later. I'm heading to work." I wave as I head out the door. Jamie is an aspiring author, so she can work from home when she's not bartending to make a little extra money. Luckily for her, her family funds her dreams and her rent. I am, unfortunately, not that lucky. I lost my mother in a car wreck about six years ago now. My dad and I are close, but he's not able to take care of both of us, which is fine. He's done enough for me. I'm a grown woman. I can take care of myself. That reminds me, I should probably call him soon. It's getting closer to Christmas, and I want to go up to our family cabin for the holiday.

I get to work at quarter after six. I slide my security card through the reader and wait for the green button to light up and the door to click, showing it's open. I walk into the office where Jace, my supervisor, is the only other one in this early.

"Morning, Jace," I call out as I walk to the other side of the floor and into my cubicle.

"Hey," he says, sparing me a mere glance. I don't take offense. Being the supervisor of the cyber security department at Hutchens & Co Security is an incredibly stressful position, and I don't envy him at all. I take a seat at my desk and boot up my computers. While I wait, I fix myself another cup of coffee and take it back to my desk.

I log into our system and check for any additional client requests before going back to the anti-hack firewall I've been building for the past six months. Once it's finished, it will hopefully put Hutchens & Co Security on the map. As far as cyber security goes, big businesses will beg for us to represent them. Well, that's the hope, at least.

I've been working here for three and a half years now, and it's pretty much my dream job. I love the challenge that it presents and the chance to always improve things and make them better. Plus, it's something I enjoy, so I can't complain. I was even able to improve their original firewall two years ago. It felt great to show my skills and be seen as a valued member on the team. As a girl in a male-dominated field, it tends to make guys think I was just here for my looks, that I didn't earn my position by skill.

I get lost in programing and coding for the next nine hours. By the time I look up, I see everyone is packing up to leave. Holy shit. I take my glasses off and rub my eyes as I realize I've been staring at the screen non-stop. Putting my glasses back on, I grab my jacket and keys before logging off.

Jace comes over and stands over my cubicle. "Great job today, Aleice. I checked in on your progress on that firewall. You're doing a great job."

I smile. Jace has always made sure I didn't feel uncomfortable around all the guys and made a point to tell me if I did a good job. I appreciate it. It's nice to feel important and to be validated in my work. He was pretty attractive too, with his sandy blond hair and his boy-next-door look. If he wasn't my boss, I might have made a move by now, but I have a strict no co-workers' policy. It just makes things so messy.

"Thanks, Jace, I appreciate it." I smile and he nods before heading back to his desk to grab his laptop and pack up for the night. Once my computer is off, I head back out toward the door. "Night." I wave as I head past Jace's desk.

He smiles. "Night."

I get in the car and crank up the heat, thinking about what I want for dinner. I send Jamie a text to see if she made anything or wants me to pick something up. Then I call my dad.

"Hey, sugarbug. How are you?" I can hear his smile down the line.

"Hey dad, I'm doing pretty good. How are you?"

"Ahhh, I'm all right. Hangin' in there. Betty down at the diner says hi."

I chuckle. Of courses he's at the diner. He's there most nights. If I didn't know any better, I'd say he and Betty have a thing going on, but I know my dad would never date again. My mother was the love of his life.

"Tell her I said hello and to not let you have the pie, you need to watch your blood sugar," I say loudly enough, hoping she overhears. I hear a soft chuckle in the background, showing she did.

"Now why in the blazes would you tell her that? That's the only reason I come to this damn diner," he says, and I hear her clear her throat. "And you, of course, Betty, that goes without sayin'."

I hear a "mmhmm" before she must have walked away.

"Damnit, now I'm really not getting any pie," he grumbles. I laugh at his misfortune, but am also grateful because he really needs to watch his blood sugar.

"So, I was thinking of heading to the cabin in a few weeks for Christmas. I wanted to check in and see if you wanted to go with me?" I know I'm pushing my luck with this. Dad never goes to the cabin anymore. It reminds him too much of mom, but he can't get rid of it for the same reason. I have so many happy memories there. I love that cabin, it's my happy place. Nestled in the woods on Kilburn Mountain, about five hours north of here.

"Ah, thanks, sugar, but I think I'm going to have to pass this year. Maybe next year." He says the same thing every year, and every year he comes up with some sort of excuse.

"All right dad, no problem. I will drop by on my way up through to give you your Christmas gift."

"You don't have to do that; you know I don't want or need nothin'." He sighs.

"I know you don't, but I enjoy getting you something, so let me," I respond with only a little attitude. "All right, well, I'm going to head home from work. I will talk to you later, okay? Love you."

"Allright sugarbug, drive safe and I love you too," he says before hanging up the phone.

Now that the car is nice and warm, I check my phone for a text from Jamie. She says she made dinner. So I head straight home.

CHAPTER 4

Shaw

The next week goes by, and I can't stop thinking about Aleice. All my thoughts turn back to her. It's a distraction I'm not used to having. So finally, I cave and decide to do some research.

She's my employee. What are the odds of that? "FUCK!" I grunt, as I slam my fist down on my desk. After she left her phone number on that brief note, I used it along with her name to run a background check. What's the good of having a security company if you can't do a background check on your one-night stand?

I stand and pace around my office as I reflect on all the information I dug up on her. Her full name is Aleice Jane Taylor, she's 28, her mom passed away in a car accident six years ago, her dad lives in New York in a little condo just outside the city after he sold the house he had with his late wife. Aleice lives in an apartment not too far from here, with a roommate named Jamie. And she's been my goddamned employee for three and a half years, and she's damn good at her job. The firewall she helped develop two years ago has saved our ass a few times against serious security threats, and she is currently building another one that will change the game for cyber security, and when I buy it off her, which I plan to do, I can sell it to our clients as added protection and it will make me a shit ton of money.

I have a strict no fraternization policy in place. I can't date an employee. It's ridiculous that my thoughts went down that path to begin with. I have never had the desire to settle down. I've always been solely focused on work. And yet, for some reason, I was disappointed earlier when I woke up alone. I would have loved a few more rounds with her. That must be it. I just wanted more sex. The fact that she is incredibly smart, and the natural chemistry we seemed to share has nothing to do with it. I try not to let the disappointment sink in. I don't get attached. I sure as fuck don't catch feelings for one-night stands. She was just a fuck, a warm body that I needed after a hard day at work. I don't do relationships, I'm a workaholic who's married to his job.

From the ground up, I built this company and worked my ass off to get it to where it is today. After six tours of deployment, I came back with only a few scars and my high school education to show for it. The need to fight, to defend, still burning strong within me, the military sense of duty undeniable. Being a Marine is in my blood; it's so engrained in my being, I don't know how to be anything else. As a veteran, finding a job that I was qualified for was difficult, almost impossible. So, I created Hutchens & Co Security with my best buddy and fellow jarhead, Reed Connor. We hire veterans and we are damn good at our jobs. It was actually Reed's idea to offer cyber security. That's his baby, so I let him handle that entire department, including hiring and firing.

I walk back around my desk and open the drawer with the sticky note she left me, grab it and toss it into the trash beside my desk. I just won't ever call her back. It's not like I promised her anything. She knew what it was from the start.

With that settled, I sit down in my chair and get back to work. We have a few new clients that are interested in hiring our security team. I currently have a group of eight men. I can always get more as our company expands, but for now that number seems to be a good fit.

I attend a few client meetings and make a few calls to check in on my guys. I usually like to check in once a week to make sure everything is going smoothly. Most of the time everything is fine, but sometimes my men are in dangerous situations, so I like to check in personally.

After eating a quick lunch, I finish up more calls and one more client meeting before shutting down, thankful that it's Friday. I rub my forehead before running my hands through my hair. I can't get the image of Aleice out of my head. I keep picturing her sprawled out naked on my bed with her brown hair fanned out around her. Her big full breasts bouncing while she rides my cock. Fuck. I shake my head, trying to clear the images from my mind. I don't want to walk through the building with a raging hard-on. I stand from my desk and glance down at my cock extending the fly of my pants. I take several deep breaths, trying to calm myself down, before tucking my cock into my waistband.

I grab my wallet and my keys before making my way down the stairs and out the door. This industrial office building has only two floors, but it suites us well. With most of my security team either out on assignments or waiting on assignments, they don't really need a lot of space at the office. Mostly, the top floor is the HR department and Reed's and my offices. The first floor houses our tech department, where Jace manages the day-to-day, which Reed oversees.

I can't believe she's been under me this whole time. This funny, sexy, smart woman has been within reach, and I never knew it. Well, that's probably for the best because it was just one night. Get ahold of yourself, man. It was just a one-night stand. Shaking my head, I walk out into the parking lot.

I click the unlock button on my key fob and climb into my truck. Although my apartment is high end and flashy, I much prefer the simple and quiet. That's why I have my cabin in upstate New York, right on Kilburn Mountain. I like the seclusion it provides, not having any neighbors for miles—it reminds me of simpler times. Sure, I may have good money now, but it wasn't always like this, and the Marine in me likes things simple. It's where I can go to get away, where I don't have to hold this façade of rich CEO. I can just simply be.

As I think about it, I make a mental note to head up there for the holidays. It will be a much-needed break. I haven't taken a day off in over two years. A nice long vacation is definitely due. I blink and realize I somehow drove all the way home without realizing it, as if in a trance, just driving on autopilot. I park my truck in the underground lot and get into the elevator, swiping my keycard to access my penthouse suite.

The doors close and seconds later, the elevator rises, the numbers for the floors zipping by. At the top, the doors open, and I walk out into my apartment. Looking around, I picture Aleice's face when she first saw it, the awe and amazement clear in her expression as she took in its opulence. I try to see it through her eyes, taking in the high ceilings and the expensive masculine furniture. It is nice, but it's also not home. There are no personal touches that mark it as mine. It's just a house, a place to lay my head.

Jesus Christ, when did I get so damn sentimental? First the... dare I say disappointment that Aleice is an employee and not something I can even remotely entertain, even if I wanted to? Which I *don't*. Then there's this feeling of emptiness in my home that, for a short time, seemed to be absent with her presence. Fuck this.

I walk further into the open space and shrug my jacket off before tossing it over the back of one of the chairs in the living room, and then tugging on the knot in my tie. Once it's loose enough, I take it over my head and drape it onto the chair with my jacket. I blow out a breath as I walk over to the liquor cabinet in the corner of the living room. Opening the door, I take out the Jameson and a glass, dropping an ice ball into the glass and pouring the Jameson in. I take a sip slowly, letting the liquor glide down my throat, enjoying the spicy flavor burn as it hits the back of my tongue, the hint of vanilla as it finishes.

I sit down in one of the club chairs closest to the fireplace and press the button to turn it on. Leaning back in the chair, I cross my ankle over my other knee, resting the glass where they meet. I try to focus on where the company is heading, how in the last two years the company has expanded and is steadily exceeding profit projections that we had run at the beginning of the year. As I continue to run the numbers though my head, I think about how much money Aleice's new hack-proof program will bring in. The girl is a genius. I can't help the smirk, a small sense of pride at that thought. I take another sip of my drink and look around my silent apartment. Never has the silence bothered me before, but now as I sit here alone, I can't help but feel lonely. I down the rest of my drink before getting up, turning off all the lights, and heading to the kitchen to put my glass in the sink. In my bedroom, I unbutton and shrug off my shirt before undoing and removing my pants. I put them in the laundry basket for the housekeeper to bring to the dry cleaner's tomorrow.

I walk into the en suite bathroom before turning on the shower with the sauna feature, needing the heat to loosen my tense muscles. After climbing in, I let my head drop back between my shoulders as the waterfall showerhead rains down over my head and body, slowly loosening the tension that has been building up in my body since I found out Aleice works for me. My shoulders droop as I relax into it. Remaining still for a few moments, I grab the shampoo and lather it up before washing my hair. As I reach for the body wash, my thoughts turn to Aleice unbidden. The image is vibrant in my mind of her soft pink folds glistening with arousal as she moans for me. I can still hear the sound as it echoes in my mind. My cock stiffens at the thought, and I can't help but reach down and squeeze myself from root to tip, enjoying the slight sting and the pleasure it brings, reminding me of how tight her perfect little pussy is. I stroke myself faster as I remember her eyes as she called me daddy, the shock but also the desire that was behind that one word. The desire to have me take charge and take care of her, the desire to be controlled and dominated. I groan at the thought of her body, languid and soft under me, the thought of doing anything I want to her and her willingly begging for it. I imagine her bent over, that sexy round ass in the air as my mouth feasts on her beautiful opening. The sounds of her desire still ringing in my ears. Fuck. I rest my arm on the shower wall as my legs weaken slightly, as images assault my mind of her amazing curves and her body writhing and squirming for me. The way her legs shook before she squirted all over my face. The taste of her sweetness that lingered long after I was done. I explode as my orgasm tingles along my spine and down my legs. Jet after jet releasing over my hand and the shower wall. I rest my head on the cold tile as I catch my breath and get my bearings. What is this girl doing to me? I run my hand down my face as I release a harsh breath before rinsing myself off and turning off the water. I dry off and crawl into bed, knowing tomorrow is another day and I won't allow her to enter my head again. This was one day of weakness, that's it. Tomorrow I will hit the gym and work her out of my system for good. I close my eyes and let myself drift off to sleep.

Before I know it, my alarm is going off and I look over to see it's already four in the morning. Shutting off the alarm, I roll out of bed, ambling over to my closet to grab a t-shirt and shorts. I grab my sneakers and begin getting dressed. I run a brush through my hair before brushing my teeth and grabbing my keys. I head down to the basement where there is a full-size gym.

I start off with a run to warm up before I hit the weights. Every time my thoughts drift to Aleice, I do another rep, punishing my muscles for my wandering mind. After two hours, my muscles are screaming, and I know I'm going to be paying for this in a few days. After heading back to my apartment, I drink a post-workout and protein shake. I usually work out of my in-home office on the weekends just to check in and make sure everything is still running smoothly.

After taking a quick shower to rid myself of all the sweat, I throw on a clean t-shirt and a pair of jeans, before making my way to my office do some work. A few hours in, my cell phone rings.

"Hey Reed, how's it going?" I answer, recognizing the number.

"Not good. We have a security breach."

My mind blanks as I try to process what he's saying. "But that's not possible. Our servers are practically hack-proof," I answer, disbelief in my voice.

He takes a deep breath before continuing. "The threat was from within." He drops the bomb and we both sit in silence, realizing what this means.

"Who?" I ask, seething. Who could have the balls to fuck with my company, and try to do it under my nose? I pant as I try to get my anger under control.

"We don't know with a hundred percent certainty, but we have a suspect... Aleice Taylor."

My mind blanks as I process the betrayal. She must have known who I was the whole time, playing innocent as she laughed behind my back at the stupid CEO who fucked her while she fucked with his company. I see red as I practically foam at the mouth. How fucking dare she! I will ruin her! "I want her gone and I want a lawsuit brought against her. I want her to fucking rot!" I yell down the line as my rage boils over.

"We will take care of this, brother," he promises, the vow clear in his voice before disconnecting the line.

I slam the phone down. I pick up one of the vases, the interior designer *insisted* I have to add a hint of 'femininity to break up all the masculine within the space', and throw it against the wall, watching it shatter into a thousand pieces. "FUCKKK!" I roar so loud my throat burns as the sound scrapes against it. This... this right here is why I fuck women without letting feelings muddle it. Women are nothing but a warm hole. They always want something, whether it be money, or to stand on the arm of a man who has some. They are all the fucking same. My body shakes with the force of my rage. I can't remember a time when I was this angry. My vision blurs and all I see is red.

I spin around and slam my fist through the wall, angry that I let her get to me. How could I have even entertained the idea of having feelings for her? Stupid. Fucking stupid. I walk over to my safe and quickly enter the code before I hear the click. I open the door and pull out my SIG P320, shoving it in the back of my waistband before grabbing ammo and slamming the safe door closed.

The elevator doors open. I head out to my truck, getting in and putting the firearm in the center console with the ammo before turning the truck on and heading out to the range. My body shakes with uncontrollable rage. I need a place to unleash this anger, and the best place I can think of is the range, or else I might do something that could get me twenty-five to life. She will pay for this. I'll make fucking sure of it!

CHAPTER 5

Aleice

Thank God for the weekend. After going for a run and hitting the shower, I sit in my small, cramped living room on my hand-me-down couch with a book. Staring at a computer all day gets redundant. I need the break from the constant strain on my brain. Just letting myself get lost in the words of someone else's imagination. Sprawling out on the couch with my fuzzy socks and my oversized sweater. I reach over and grab my coffee cup off the table and take a sip, enjoying the full-bodied flavor and the warmth as it hits my belly. I groan softly at the taste. God, I love coffee.

Glancing around my small apartment, I think about how much money I'm going to make with the program I'm developing. Soon I'll be able to get out of this dump and into something nicer. Not as grand as Shaw's, but at least bigger than the size of one of his closets. The thought of Shaw brings a sense of longing. Why hasn't he called me? I thought we had a great night and were really hitting it off. Maybe I misread the signals. Maybe he really did just want one night of sex, and was so smooth about it that I read more into it. I shake my head; I shouldn't keep letting him creep into my mind, but I can't help it. He was such a force, the air of confidence and how he commanded a room without even trying. It was such a turn on. The way he took charge and controlled my body, bringing me to unmeasurable pleasure.

I grunt. It was just a one-night stand. He will not call you. He got what he wanted and to be honest, so did I. I needed the good sex, so I should just appreciate it for what it is. I pick my book back up and continue reading.

The weekend ends too soon. My alarm blares, signaling it's 6 a.m. already. Shutting off the alarm, I slowly drag open my weary eyes and stretch my arms, enjoying the feeling of my muscles unfurling after a restless night. I have this weird uneasy feeling slowly growing in my gut, like shit is about to hit the fan. I shake off the feeling and get dressed before making myself a travel mug of coffee.

I walk through the office doors at five till seven and the unnerving feeling gets stronger as I notice everyone glance over at me as I walk to my desk. What is going on? I just put my bag down when I see Jace's shadow hanging over my desk. I look up to see a serious look on his face.

"I need to speak with you right now," he says, aggravation lacing his tone. He walks away, and I quickly follow him, expecting him to turn into one of the conference rooms that we usually use for conferences or self-isolation to focus. Instead, he continues to the stairway, heading upstairs.

Oh, shit. My heart races as fear sinks in, causing my stomach to clench and nausea to rise. What the fuck is going on? I've never been in trouble before. The only time I've ever even been up to the second floor was when I first got hired on and needed to fill out my paperwork. We enter Jessica's office—the head of HR.

She glances up as we walk through the door, a slight frown on her face. "Please have a seat, Miss. Taylor."

I cringe slightly as I take a seat. "I'm sorry, but what is this about? Am I in trouble?" I sit on my trembling hands, my leg bouncing anxiously. I'm scared. Before she has a chance to answer, the door is thrown open and Shaw comes through, looking like he's ready to kill. My eyes widen in shock. How is he here? Did he know I work here? What on earth is going on! Am I in trouble for having a one-night stand? No, they can't get mad at me about that. I stare at him in pure confusion, glancing between Jace and Jessica searching for answers. Anything to make this situation make sense.

He lets out a humorless chuckle. "Oh, like you didn't know," Shaw sneers, his tone menacing.

My eyes widen into saucers before my brows furrow so hard I can barely see. "I'm sorry. Can someone please tell me what's going on? I have literally never been more confused in my life." I swallow down the bile slowly rising in my throat. Fear—so thick I'm practically choking on it as it grips my stomach and tightens into knots.

"Drop the act. We all know you did it," Shaw all but yells, his face turning a light shade of pink with anger.

I shake my head, still not on the same page. Hell, I'm pretty sure I'm not even in the same book. "I have no idea what's going on, can someone please explain to me what's happening?" I screech out in panic.

Clearing her throat, Jessica stands and takes over the direction of the conversation. "Miss Taylor, we called you in here today to let you know you are terminated, and we will be presenting you with a lawsuit regarding the money and information you have stolen from our clients."

My eyebrows jump up to my hairline at the absurdity of what she is saying.

"Our clients come to us for security, Miss Taylor, we can't have you messing with, not only our company, but also the safety of companies that trust us."

My mouth drops open but before I can even form a rebuttal, two huge hulking men come in and stand next to me, not touching me but certainly making it known what their intentions are.

"You will be forcefully removed from the premises, and if we ever catch you near our company again, we will have you arrested onsite. You are lucky we don't have you arrested right now." Jess lifts her lip in disgust at me.

Hulk to the right growls as he tosses my bag onto my lap and says, "Up." I stand and, with one last sad look at Shaw, I head out the door with Thing One and Thing Two close behind to escort me all the way to my car. Fuck.

After I get home, I strip out of my clothes and put on my pjs, wallowing in self-pity for a while. How could they possibly think I did that? Why would I when I was building a huge program that would make me more money than I could ever steal from any of the clients? Plus, I helped make the firewall to protect all their information. Why would I make it just to help myself two years later? Fuck, none of this makes any sense. And what was Shaw doing there? After pacing a hole in the rug in my living room, I throw myself onto the couch. When did a one-night stand get so difficult? I sigh as I rub my temples to ease the oncoming headache. I just lost my job and I'm being sued. I shake my head as the tears burn my eyes. I have a little nest egg that I've been saving up, but it won't last long.

I have to find a way to prove my innocence. I'm not sure why someone would want to frame me for this. God, nothing makes sense. I close my eyes, suddenly exhausted. This is going to be a long week.

* * *

It's five thirty on Thursday and I'm getting ready to head to the cabin for the weekend. Tomorrow is Christmas Eve, and I decided to head up early. Plus, it's not like I have to worry about work. I sniff and wipe away the stray tear. I take a deep breath. No, I promised myself I was done crying and done being sad. The truth will come out. I will find a way to get the truth out, to clear my name. Plus, I still have my program—which I've been working on—that I can sell in order to make enough money to never work again.

As I head out of town, I stop by dad's little condo. I glance around as I get out of my car, feeling the ever-present weight of eyes. Always there, always watching. I shake my head and knock on the door, waiting for dad to answer.

"Hey, sugarbug. Come in, come in," he says as he opens the door and moves aside to let me by.

"Hey dad. Thanks." I walk in and take off my jacket, hanging it up on the hook by the front door.

"How's work been?"

I cringe before turning around so he can't see my face. "It's going well, you know, same ol', same ol'," I tell him, feeling bad for lying, but I don't want him to worry.

"Good, good." He smiles as he walks over to his recliner and plops himself down. I glance around the small, cozy place.

I shake my head and smile. "Merry Christmas," I say as I hand him the present I've been holding.

He furrows his brows. "Sugar, I told you I don't need nothin'. You didn't have to do that." He shakes his head.

"I know I didn't have to, but I wanted to. Someone's got to take care of you." I smile.

He takes his time opening up the present.

"I know it's not much..." I frown slightly, wishing I could give him more. He's been so good to me the last six years since we lost mom. He's been my rock, and I don't know if I would have survived without him.

He finally gets it open to find a universal remote. He gives me a strange look. "Thanks bug."

I burst out laughing, tears streaming down my face. He thinks I just wrapped a TV remote and gave it to him. I wipe at my eyes as I tell him, "It's a universal remote, meaning you can use it for everything instead of that." I point at his coffee table, where there are six different remotes.

"Ahh... okay, that makes more sense." He smiles and I walk him through the setup and how to use it.

He stands from his chair with a grunt and pulls me into a big bear hug. I can't help but smile as I squeeze him back.

"Love you, dad." I say into his barrel chest.

"Love you too, bug."

Once he releases me, he walks over to the small, sad Charlie Brown-looking tree in the corner of the room and grabs a gift from underneath it. With another grunt, he stands and walks back over to me before finally handing it over. "Merry Christmas."

I shake my head. "Dad, you didn't need to get me anything. You know you should be saving your money!" I scolded him slightly with a disgruntled look on my face.

"Oh, shut up and let your old man give you something."

I purse my lips but smile slightly as I open the wrapping paper, then the box. Inside is a beautiful, soft green cashmere scarf. My eyes widen as I take it in. "Oh my gosh, dad, this is way too expensive," I say as I drop the box and hug the scarf to my chest.

He just smirks. "It's not like I have anyone else to spend my money on. Why not spoil my girl?"

My shoulders droop as I stare at my dad. How did I get so lucky? "Thank you, dad, so much," I sniffle, trying to hold back the tears.

"Oh, don't do that bug. It's just a damn scarf."

A laugh bursts out of me and I hug him again. "Thank you again."

He just nods and kisses me on my head.

"Okay, now it's time to make some dinner." I look at him as I head towards the kitchen. I raid his cabinets until I find all the ingredients I need to make stuffed shells. Before too long, the house starts to smell delicious and dad's nose gets the better of him and he ambles his way into the kitchen.

"Hmm, something smells good."

I smile as I make my way around the little kitchen.

"You must get this from your mom. God knows I can't cook to save my life." He chuckles softly as he looks at me with such fondness.

Taking a deep breath, I let a small smile touch my face at the thought of her. It's times like this that make it difficult to think of her. Not having her around for the holidays kills me, but I know she's in a better place and that's what I hold on to—knowing she's looking down on us and keeping us safe.

Once dinner is all served up, we sit at his modest two-person table and eat. It's mostly silent as dad chows down like it's his last meal.

"Okay, slow down before you choke," I laugh. "I obviously need to come around more often and cook you some more meals." I reach out and rest my hand on his. "I'm sorry I haven't been around a lot lately."

He makes a fart noise with his mouth. "Oh, I'm fine. I know you've got your own life, doing all those computery things."

I smirk. "But that's not an excuse. I can always make time for you. I'm sorry I've been so wrapped up in my own little world."

He shakes his head. "Don't worry, kid, it happens. I'm always here."

I squeeze his hand in acknowledgement, and we go back to eating. When dinner's done, I clear the table and wash the dishes for him. "Bug, you don't have to do that," he chastises.

"I know, it's fine. I enjoy helping out." I smile at him as I dry the dishes and put them away. "All right, I'm going to head out. I still have a long drive to Kilburn."

He nods his head. "Okay, bug. You drive safe now. Watch the roads, it's getting cold out there. It'll be even colder on the mountain. Watch for ice."

I roll my eyes. "I'll be okay. I'll drive safe.

Promise." I lean in and give him a hug and a kiss on the cheek. "Love you."

"Love you too, bug." He waves me off as I exit the front door and head down the steps to my car. Getting in, I crank up the heat and wrap my scarf tighter around my neck.

"Fuck, it's cold as tits in here," I mumble to myself as I shiver. Making sure there is no one coming, I pull out of the parallel parking spot and make my way to the interstate.

It's dark by the time I'm thirty minutes out from the cabin. As I make my way up the mountain, I notice the roads are getting slick, so I drive slower. As I come up to a big turn, I feel my wheels skid out from under me, and I slide toward the edge of the road. I try to adjust, but my wheels get no traction, and I slide off the road and down into a ditch before slamming into a enormous oak tree. My head bounces off the steering wheel, then cracks into my side window. I feel the warm blood as it trickles down the side of my face like tears. My vision fades. I try to breathe deep and keep myself awake. The fear of passing out alone, on the side of the road in the dark, only works so long to starve off the fading darkness. I feel the blood soaking through my shirt before my eyes close for good.

CHAPTER 6

Shaw

It's late by the time I finally leave work. I've spent all day trying to do damage control with our clients while also trying to get all the money back that Aleice had stolen. So far, we haven't been able to find the money, but I'm not too surprised by that. The girl is too smart to hide it out in the open. To be honest, I'm surprised it was so easy to catch her. We have some talented guys on our cyber team, and they made sure to track her down.

As I turn the last corner up Kilburn to my cabin, I notice my truck lights show skid marks on the road. I think little of it until I follow them and see a car almost folded around a tree.

"Holy shit!" I slam the truck in park and jump out, my Marine training kicking in. I quickly assess the area and make sure that it's safe. I smell gas but I don't see any fire, but it doesn't mean one won't start. The driver's side door is blocked, so I head to the passenger's side. The door is locked. Without thinking, I slam my fist through the window. Adrenaline running so high I don't feel a thing... yet. I unlock it and wrench the door open, and half-crawl inside. I see blood all over the side window and down a woman's chest. Fuck, she's really hurt. "Ma'am, my name is Shaw and I'm here to help. Are you all right? Are you able to talk to me?" I continue to speak, hoping it might wake her up without touching her. If she has any neck injuries, I don't want to move her. She makes a pained moan, so I know she's alive. I can't see her face beyond the matted blood-soaked hair. I look around. I can't leave her here with the temperature continuing to drop, and being this far out, an ambulance may not make it in time. She could bleed out. I can't see how much damage she has sustained.

I have medical supplies at my cabin, and it's only three minutes away. With the decision made, I take out my pocketknife and cut off her seatbelt. "Ma'am, I'm going to get you out of here. Okay, stay with me."

She groans. I position my body so I'm able to lift her weight without falling forwards, and I slide my arm under her legs as smoothly as I can, then slide my left arm under her back before lifting her into my arms. I lean my shoulder against her head, so it doesn't jostle while I move her. Pulling her free from the car, I walk back to mine and open the door before placing her into the seat. "Hold on, sweetheart. You're going to be okay." I try to soothe her as she makes small, pained noises.

Getting back into the driver's seat, I take off to my cabin. I drive slowly so I don't disturb her anymore than necessary. I pull the truck right up to the front porch and quickly unlock the door before going back and carrying her inside.

Carrying her tiny body over to the leather couch, I slowly lower her down and run to grab my medical kit, rushing back to get to work.

I kneel beside her and brush her hair away from her face in order to access the wound. When I see her face, my hand stops. My breath gets knocked from my chest. It's Aleice. I stop, just a brief moment of hesitation where my mind is at war with itself. The Marine in me says it doesn't matter who she is—it's a life and I need to protect it. And the rest of me hates this woman for trying to destroy my company and all the hard work I've put into building it for the last four years. Shaking my head, I get back to work. She can live and rot in jail. I clean up the large gash on her forehead and on the side of her head, doing my best to clean off as much of the blood as I can. She grumbles, still mostly unconscious. The gash on the side of her head could really use stitches, but with no numbing or pain medicine, I'm not sure that's the best idea. I end up getting super glue and gluing it closed. Not the best, but it will work for now. Once she's all done, I load wood into the wood stove to warm the cabin up a bit. I quickly clean and wrap my hand that I used to smash open her car window. Then I head outside, needing to get my anger under control now that the immediate danger is taken care of.

Walking outside for some fresh air, I can still smell her flowery perfume. I grab my hair in my hands and pull. "Fuck," I growl out. So many conflicting emotions overwhelming my system, anger being the most predominant. I can't deny that there was fear as well. She could have died if I hadn't come along. Even if she could stop the bleeding on her head, her car wouldn't run. With the freezing temperature, she would have caught hypothermia. She could have called for help, but with the shoddy cell service on the mountain, there is no guarantee she could reach anyone.

I shake my head. I shouldn't care. *This bitch stole from you*, I reprimand myself. She fucked you and was laughing behind your back at how stupid you were. I pace back and forth on the deck as I try to process it all. It's then I feel the snow that's melting instantly on my heated skin. Glancing around, I notice there is already about an inch on the ground, and it continues to fall fast. After about ten minutes, I hear a small voice from inside.

"Hello?"

I take one last deep breath before heading back inside to address the situation. "Hey," I say as I walk in behind her. Her head whips around and her eyes go wide before she topples over. Instinctually I reach forward and catch her. "Don't make any sudden movements. You lost quite a bit of blood and you probably have a concussion," I growl out, my anger bleeding into my voice.

She whimpers, and I'm not sure if it's from my tone or the pain. She takes a steadying breath and steps away. Looking around, I see her brows furrow in confusion, creasing the minor cut in her nose that she got from her glasses during the wreck.

"We are at my cabin," I say, answering her unspoken question. I walk into the kitchen and gab her a glass of juice. She follows slowly behind me. Once poured, I hand her the glass, and she takes it gratefully.

I nod my head to the wall of windows on my A-frame cabin, just on the other side of the living room. "Snow's really coming down. It looks like we are going to be trapped her for a bit." I grunt, and I see her cringe. "I have a spare bedroom down at the end of the hall. Mine is upstairs, so we won't have to see each other."

She looks away and I hear a soft sniff. "All right, well, thank you for helping me and for not throwing me out in the snow," she attempts a joke, but it falls flat. She just nods her head and head off down the hall to the spare bedroom.

What the fuck am I going to do now? I rest my hands on the concrete countertop of my island, dropping my head between my arms. "Merry fucking Christmas," I mumble to myself.

CHAPTER 7

Aleice

How did I end up here? I sit on the bed of the cozy guest room in what appears to be my dream cabin. The beautiful A-frame with a wall of windows and high ceilings, at least twenty feet tall. It's rustic and masculine, but cozy and warm, with the wood stove warming the home. There are personal touches here that he didn't have in his penthouse. Pictures of him and his fellow jarheads posing in front of a Humvee. His smile is wide, and you can tell they are all close. This place is done up so differently from the penthouse, not dressed up fancy by an interior designer; this place was all him. With the leather couches and concrete, it's absolutely stunning and suits him much better. Looking around the space, I see it's a large room painted a light gray color with white linens on the bed and a few framed pictures on the wall of the mountain. An en suite bathroom on the right side of the room has more concrete countertops and an oak vanity. The tile is charcoal colored and ties the entire space together. A large shower takes up half the other wall in the bathroom.

I take a deep breath as I think about the situation I am in. Gently reaching up to touch the side of my head, I wince when I feel the deep inch and a half cut just above my ear. I glance up at the ceiling and whisper, "What did I do that was so wrong that you hate me this much?" speaking to the powers that be. How is it I'm stuck with a man who hates my guts for something that I didn't do, the same man who has haunted my dreams since the night he literally fucked my brains out? I palm my face as I think about it. It's probably best to just stay out of his way. Just stay in the guest room until the snow passes, then I can call my dad to come and get me and get my car towed to the repair shop—that is, if it isn't totaled.

Fuck, how am I going to pay for that? Shit, I look around now, realizing I don't have my bags or any of my belongings. I rush out the door and back into the living area to look for Shaw. "Shaw?" I ask tentatively as I reach the living room. He's nowhere to be seen. I glance around, hoping that

I just missed my things, that they are just on the floor somewhere. Nope. Of course not. I roll my eyes, and glance down at my bloody clothes and cringe.

"What?" I hear as I turn and glance up at the loft where Shaw is standing, looking over the railing.

I wince at his tone. "I'm sorry to bother you... but did you happen to grab any of my bags?" I pull out the hem of my shirt to show I need something else to wear.

He rubs the back of his neck. "No, I was busy trying to save your life," he huffs.

I wince again. "It's okay, I get it." I go to walk back toward the room, thinking I will figure something out.

"Hold on." He turns around and walks away. After a few moments, he returns and tosses a white t-shit and a pair of sweats down to me.

I catch them and give him a soft smile. "Thank you."

"Mmhm," he grunts as he walks back to his room. I head back to the guest room and the shower. Looking at myself in the mirror, I can see the crusted blood on my face and my matted hair. I turn on the water and strip down while I wait for it to warm up. Climbing in, I wash all the remaining blood off my skin and hair, enjoying the comfort that the warm water brings. I could have died tonight, if it weren't for Shaw. Why would he save me? The look of pure hatred so strong in his eyes. I cringe as I think about it. Whatever the reason, I'm glad he did.

After getting out and drying off, I put on the t-shirt Shaw gave me and it hits a few inches above my knee—I'm 5'4 to his 6'2, plus he's built like a brick shithouse. I try not to think about how gorgeous he is, and how his muscles rippled when he took control of me that night. I shake my head. Stop thinking about it, it will never happen again, especially now because I'm pretty sure he regrets saving my life. I try to put the sweatpants on, but they are so long they extend a foot past my feet, and I can't even cinch the waist tight enough to prevent them from falling off. Yeah, that will not work. Foregoing the pants, figuring I'll just be in my room anyway, I snuggle into bed and try to get some much-needed rest. It's really late and my body is sore from being tossed around like a rag doll in the wreck.

I wake up the next morning at about six, my muscles stiff and sore. "God, it all hurts," I groan as I try to sit up. Making my way to the bathroom, I look for a pain reliever but come up empty. Slowly, I make my way out to the open kitchen-living room. Trying to be quiet, I dig through the cabinets for medicine until I finally find the Advil.

"Oh, thank God," I mumble. Grabbing a glass of water, I take four.

Looking around, I see no sign of Shaw. That's probably for the best. We don't need anymore awkward interactions. Noticing that the coffee maker is on, I pour myself a mug and head back to the room.

After about five hours I get really bored and wander around the cabin. The door across from mine is an office. My fingers itch to get on the computer, but I refrain, not needing any more reasons for Shaw to hate me. I make my way out to the living room and I see a bookshelf behind the couch filled to the brim with books. My eyes light up. I make my way over and look through. Most of them are business related, but there are some Tom Clancy books in the bunch. I choose one of those to grab; there is no way I'm bored enough to read a textbook. I take it back to my room. I continue to read all the Tom Clancy books he has in his collection over the next four days. I see or hear nothing from Shaw whatsoever.

On the fifth day, I'm getting stir crazy and need human interaction, even if it's with a man I promised myself I wouldn't speak to. I have to keep a shield up. I've got to remember he hates me.

I make my way out to the living room and see Shaw sitting on the couch watching TV with a large mug of coffee in his hand.

"Morning," I hedge as I make my way toward him, still wearing the t-shirt he gave me. I've been showering daily and hand washing my underwear in the sink, and luckily there was a deodorant in the bathroom, so at least I don't stink.

He glances over his shoulder and his brows drop as if just remembering I was here. His eyes drop as he takes in my legs and his jaw clenches. Suddenly self-conscious, I pull the hem down even though you can't see anything. I slowly walk forward, not sure what else to say. I figure the best way to get on someone's good side is through food, right? Isn't the saying, the way to friendship is through the stomach? Well, it is now. I turn right and walk into the kitchen and start pulling out the eggs and bacon and all the other ingredients for a frittata. Grabbing the cast-iron skillet, I get to work in silence.

At some point, I see Shaw, out of the corner of my eye, approach the island and watch me, probably worried I will poison him. I roll my eyes as I put the pan in the oven. Wiping my hands off on the dish towel, I turn around. "Should be ready in about twenty minutes."

He tilts his head to the side, assessing me before he nods. I turn back around, unable to stand under his scrutiny, and get a cup of coffee. When that's done, I look out the window and see the snow is now blocking half of the view from it.

Shaw sees me looking and says, "Yeah, and we are supposed to be getting another six feet."

My jaw drops open. We could be stuck here for at least another week. It's not uncommon to get quite a bit more snow up in the mountains, but this much is crazy.

"I know you hate me, but can we at least talk? I have so many questions and seeing as we can't go anywhere…" I gesture to the snow.

He growls low in his throat. "I have nothing to say to you. You fucked with my company, with my livelihood, you're as good as dead to me." His harsh sneer makes me wince.

Then I think about what he said. "Wait, your company?" My eyes widen as I realize what he's saying. His brows furrow at my confusion as his head jerks back. "Hutchens… holy fuck," I say as a few of the puzzle pieces click together.

He tilts his head, truly looking at me. "You either really didn't know, or you should be up for an Oscar." He rubs his forehead before running his hand through his hair. "You really had no clue, did you?" he says, disbelief in his voice.

"I swear I had no idea." I look him directly in his eyes, begging him to believe me. "I have no clue what was even going on."

He rolls his eyes and turns his back on me. "I can't believe that. We have evidence that your credentials were used to get into twelve different clients' accounts."

I cough and sputter into my coffee cup. "You WHAT?!" I ask once I stop choking on my coffee. "That makes no sense." I stare at the ground like it's going to give me all the answers to the insanity that's unfolding in front of me.

He turns around, finally making eye contact.

"Okay, so don't take this the wrong way, but if I were to hack into the system and steal from the clients, I sure as hell wouldn't use my login. Shit, I'd just hack my way through the back door I made for edits in the firewall, and I'd be able to access their accounts through the clients that were set up for autopay via their bank information. Or I could trace any one of our clients' IP addresses and install a keystroke malware and just get the bank login that way. Shit, now that I think about it, there are a lot of ways I could..." I cringe when I realize I just stuck my foot in my mouth. "Sorry... what I'm trying to say is, if I wanted to steal from the clients, there is no way you would know it was me. I could hack into the government alphabet agencies right now, with minor effort, but I have no desire to do that. I would much rather be on the protection side than on the hacking side. But in order to know how to protect, I also have to know how to hack." I shrug. He stares at me for so long I get uncomfortable and I wring my hands together.

CHAPTER 8

Shaw

"Show me," I grit out between my teeth as I walk towards my in-home office. I don't even look behind me to make sure she is following me; I know she's there. Holding the door open, I wait for her to walk through before closing it behind her. She looks at my setup and nods to herself before walking over and taking a seat.

"Would you like to log in or do you want me to hack into that too, to prove myself to you?" she says with a hint of mirth in her eyes.

I walk over and enter my password to open

access to the computers. She takes a deep breath and cracks her knuckles before she types, so fast I can hardly see what she is doing. Screens pop up and close quickly before she finally gets to where she wants. She appears to be entering code before she enters our system at Hutchens & Co. My jaw drops as she goes through our system at light-speed. I had them beef it up after she left to avoid this happening again and she is literally working our system over like a preschooler playing with blocks.

"Huh," she says as she reads through and continues to dive deep into the system.

"Huh, what?" I growl out, not liking that she can access so easily, nor that she's not telling me what the fuck is going on.

"Give me a second. I'm getting closer to fig-uring out exactly who hacked the system and what they did. I have my suspicions, but I need to con-firm because I'm not going to throw people under the bus without being certain."

Her jab doesn't go unnoticed. I rub my fore-head as I pace back and forth.

"Fuck!" she growls. Suddenly, the screens go completely black.

"What the fuck is happening?" I ask. "What the fuck did you do!" I see words appear on the screen. Holy shit, it's like something out of a movie. I glance at Aleice, expecting to see shock on her face. Instead, I see her roll her eyes so hard I'm pretty sure her right eye gets lost in the back of her skull.

She scoffs. "Fucking noob, why are the villains always so dramatic?"

"Aleice, what the fuck is happening?!"

"He knows. I was about to put a tracer on him, and he blocked me out of the system. I can hack back in easily enough through his block, but I'm curious about what he has to say. Hold on."

I watch as the words on the screen form a sentence It says '*I see you*' as if teasing us. They think this is some kind of game.

She types back. '*Good, now tell me why you framed me for this shit?*'

After a few seconds, her words disappear, and a response comes. '*Because I needed you away from him.*'

My brows furrow in confusion. "Away from who?" I ask out loud.

She types again, ignoring me. '*Why?*'

His response comes immediately '*Because you are mine!*'

My blood runs cold as I think about this psychopath coming after Aleice. Whomever it is all but admitted she had been framed. "Who is it?" I ask again.

She spins around in the chair and with a distraught look on her face says, "Jace." I can almost see puzzle pieces clicking together behind her eyes.

"What..." My eyes widen as I take in the information.

Before we can dive any deeper into that, he writes again. '*You have always been mine.*'

She shivers and a blank expression crosses her face.

"Aleice, what is going on?" I ask her, needing her to fill me in because I'm lost.

"For the past few years, I've had this feeling of being watched. It was so often I eventually got used to it and just figured it was me being paranoid since I never saw anyone. Then I started working at your company and it seemed to lessen, which confirmed it was just my imagination, or at least until after our night together. Now I feel him everywhere, always watching." She shivers and shakes her head in disbelief, quickly putting together what she was insinuating.

"So, you think Jace has been stalking you?"

She nods her head. "I mean, I don't have evidence or anything, but," she waves her hand at the computer screen, "he's clearly lost it."

"Tell me how you know Jace is the one who hacked into the accounts and framed you?" I demand, wanting to make sure I get all the information, and proof. For all I know she could be pushing the blame off on someone else. Although, I have to admit, a part of me knows that's not true. The look of shock on her face when she was fired, and then again when she found out that it was my company, that I was her boss. It was too genuine. There is no way she could have faked that.

"Okay," she says as she turns the chair back around and, after typing for a moment, the screen is back up and we have control again. "I have to work fast; he's going to keep trying to block me out." She rolls her eyes. "Stupid boy thinks he can play with me," she huffs out in a whisper. She brings up two different screens and shows me before hitting print, so we have the evidence in hand. Then she goes back to work, printing off all the evidence she can find before he takes over again. "Grrrrr," she growls out as the screen goes black again. She pushes her glasses back up her nose. I smirk slightly at how cute she is when she's frustrated, shaking the thought away as I focus back in on what's going on.

"He and I can go back and forth for days,

but I got most of the evidence printed." She walks over to my printer and grabs all the pages. "So, he has been taking pennies off the dollar from everyone's account for the last year. It's been such small amounts at a time, it's gone easily unnoticed. It's been showing up as an accounting error." She shakes her head. "It's actually pretty smart," she murmurs, to herself more than me. I clear my throat. "Right, sorry," She cringes. "Over the last six months he has been using my login to sneak into their accounts, not actually doing anything..." She points to the area on the paper. "Just making it look like I entered. Who brought you the evidence on me?" she asks as she stares at the paper.

"Jace," I growl out.

She nods her head as if expecting that. "So, he was trying to get me away from... you." She looks directly up at me. "Which makes sense. He could have kept this going for much longer, but it looks like he cut it short. Maybe since we hooked up." Her eyes open slightly as she puts the pieces together. I look to the corner of the room, not out of discomfort with the topic, but in order to think clearly and try to connect the dots here.

Talking out loud, I say, "So, he found out we hooked up that night. Feeling possessive, he sets you up to take the fall for him in order to get you away from me, and probably to make me hate you.

Then he steps in and what? Comes to your rescue?" I tilt my head. "What's his end goal here?" I say as my eyes meet hers again.

She shakes her head and shrugs. "No clue."

We stand there and stare at each other. Now that it's all out there, the tension in the room amps up. My eyes glide down her body, taking in how my shirt looks on her tiny frame, her sexy legs as she squirms under my attention.

She bites her lip. "Well, at least now you know the truth. I never betrayed you." She offers up a sad smile and turns to leave. I watch as she walks out the door. We both need the space for now, to process all we just learned.

I sink down in the computer chair and stare at the now-blank computer screen. Fucking Jace. All this time, the fucker has been right under my nose. And then he had the balls to blame Aleice for his crime. I'm so fucking angry right now. My ribs hurt from the pressure of my lungs expanding rapidly as I pant. If I ever find that motherfucker, I will kill him with my bare fucking hands. He tried to take her from me. From ME! He will never fucking get to her, never touch her if I have anything to fucking say about it. I may not know where Aleice and I stand, but I know I won't let anyone hurt her.

CHAPTER 9

Aleice

As I walk into my room, I can't help but shiver at the leftover charge that zaps through me from the tension between us. I could see the light in his eyes when he looked at me. I can't let him in again. I can't. Like I said before, I'm not good at one-night stands. I catch feelings. That's why I've been alone for so long. I have to keep the shield up or he could easily take my heart, and I'm not sure he deserves it. He was quick to blame me for something I didn't do, with little evidence. I shake my head as I lay back on the bed. Maybe keeping away will be the only way to keep my heart safe. He's so smooth, I can't let him talk his way in.

I drop down on the edge of the bed, re-moving my glasses. I rub at the rapidly-growing headache that's forming behind my eyes. Jace— this whole time it's been Jace. He's been following me for years. All this time, it wasn't my imagin-ation. I wasn't being paranoid. I shiver as I think about all the times he came over to my desk at work, took the time to talk to me about things he thought needed improved. Did I somehow lead him on? Did I make him think this was more? I run my hands through my hair. *No!* I won't let myself take the blame for other people's actions. He could have asked me out or come to me like a normal fucking person. You don't frame someone because you didn't have the balls to ask them out. Fucking psycho.

I lie back, just as I smell something burn-ing... "Fuck!" I jump up and run to the kitchen where Shaw is pulling out a fully-burnt frittata. Damn, I really wanted that frittata. "Sorry..." I whisper.

He just shakes his head. "It's fine." He gets all the ingredients out again and starts making it the exact way I had.

I tilt my head as I watch him. "You know how to make a frittata?" I mean, it's easy, but he seems more of a bacon and eggs type of guy, sim-pler things.

He chuckles slightly. "No... honestly I don't even know what it is, it just smelled good, and I watched you make it, so..."

I smirk. He was paying attention. When he misses a step, I walk over and help him. He smiles at me gratefully before putting it in the oven.

"That's an impressive memory, being able to mimic me after seeing it just once."

He shrugs off the compliment.

Needing some space, I turn around and walk into the living room to get away from his heavy presence. He has this commanding aura around him that seems to suck all the oxygen out of the room. Masculine and domineering, without even trying. Clearing my throat, I notice the news is on. I take a seat on the couch, waiting for the weather portion to come on so I can see how much longer I'm going to be stuck here. For the sake of my sanity, I hope not too long.

I twiddle my fingers together and suck at my teeth. Shit, this is awkward. What do you talk about with the guy you had a one-night stand with, then blamed you for trying to destroy his company, while also threatening to sue you? I shake my head before running my hands through my hair.

"So... this weather, yeah?" I chuckle slightly

to myself, while he turns and gives me a rueful look before heading over to the living room to sit on the opposite couch.

He rubs his hands up and down his face a few times before taking a deep breath and letting it out. "Look, I'm sorry. I should have dug deeper to confirm for sure it was you." He looks away, rubbing at his neck. "I was so pissed when I found out it could have been you after the night we spent together. I was sure that you knew who I was, and was trying to fuck me over." He shakes his head. "If I had stopped to think about it for a bit before I had reacted, I might have been able to put together that you were too smart to use your work login to access client flies."

I'm already nodding my head, my lips pursed. When he looks at me, I quickly stop and suck both my lips into my mouth. I turn away, not able to hold eye contact. Knowing if I was him, I would have been pissed too, thinking the person I had hit it off with and felt I had a great connection with had manipulated me, then stolen from me. I get where he is coming from for sure, but a part of me can't help but be a little hurt that he would think I would do that to him, that he thinks so little of me.

Looking back at him, I say, "I understand where you are coming from, and I know you don't know me well enough to determine my character, but I am not that kind of person. I want to protect people against people like that. That's the whole reason I took the job at Hutchens. I knew Reed was a veteran and that you all hired veterans. It seemed like a great company, and I wanted to be a part of it." I bite the inside of my cheek. "But what if this hadn't happened? What if we had never been trapped in here," I use my hands to gesture around us before continuing, "and you had actually taken me to court? You could have ruined my credibility with my program and destroyed my life, all over a hunch. You didn't even explain to me properly why I was being terminated, or given me a chance to defend myself." I shake my head, remembering how scared and confused I'd been over losing my job, worrying about how I was going to pay bills.

He falls back against the couch, but he remains silent. I turn to look away again, not able to let him see how much he hurt me. Finally breaking the silence, he says, "I fucked up. I'm sorry."

I look at him now, my eyes drawn to his. The level of sincerity in his voice hits me right in the chest. He stands and walks over in front of me. I look up till I finally see his face. He grabs my wrist and lifts me until I'm standing, my body flush against his, using his finger to nudge my chin up till I can see his face. As he stares into my eyes, a small smirk turns up the left side of his mouth. I bite my lip as the sight of it sends a rush of warmth straight to my core. I feel heat rush to my cheeks as my breathing picks up. Where did all the oxygen go?

His smirk turns into a full-on smile as he sees my reaction to him. Needing to get myself under control, I try to turn my head, but he holds my chin steady in his large hand. I watch as his eyes stray from mine and slide down to my lips before making their way back to my eyes. He licks his lips before leaning in and pressing them lightly against mine. I don't even have time to react before he pulls his hand free of my face and takes a step back. I instantly miss his warmth.

The timer on the oven dings, indicating the second frittata is done. I clear my throat as I try to get a handle on my feelings and the lust coursing through my body at his nearness. His confidence and dominating power sends chills through me. His tongue slides out as he licks across his top lip before drifting over the bottom one. He stares are me while he does it, like he's savoring my flavor on them. Without conscious thought, I do the same to see if I can taste him. I taste a hint of coffee and mint. I lick them again for more before biting my lip to hold in my moan.

He smirks again before returning to the kitchen to remove the frittata from the oven. I pant as I try to regulate my breathing. Now that he's far enough away from me, I can breathe. What is this guy doing to me? I need to keep my walls up. After a few deep breaths and counting to ten… twice, I walk into the kitchen, where he is cutting and plating the frittata. I take a seat at the island, and he slides the plate in front of me with a glass of orange juice.

"Thank you," I tell him as I pick up the fork and dig in. I smile big and close my eyes as I enjoy the flavor on my tongue. Delicious.

We eat in companionable silence. Occasionally, he would look down, like each bite surprised him. I cover my mouth to hide my smile. "Is it that much of a surprise?" I ask after the fourth or fifth time.

Quickly shaking his head, he says, "No, I just can't believe I made it."

I snort before covering my mouth, trying to cover the unflattering sound, praying I didn't just spray him with snot. He chuckles.

After breakfast, I go to pick up our plates to clean up the mess, but he grabs my hand. "I got it," he says. I bite the inside of my lip and nod my head. I need to get away. Before I turn to leave, I hear the meteorologist say that we should expect more snow. My eyes bulge as my feet move without instruction. I blink and I'm standing in the middle of the living room, my eyes focused on the screen. I listen as the evil man talks about a 'nor'easter' and about another two feet of snow. "No!" I say before I even realize my mouth has moved.

"Fuck." I feel his breath on the back of my neck and shivers race down my spine at the sensation. "Since my cabin is so remote, it usually doesn't even get plowed. And the road leading to the one off mine is miles out and usually the last to be done, not being a main drag."

I suck in a breath. "So, what does that mean, exactly?" I ask, wanting him to spell it out for me, even though I'm 98% sure I know exactly what he's saying.

"It means... we are most likely stuck here for at least another week." I let my head fall to my chest as I try not to cry. How am I supposed to keep my distance for another week?

"Awesome," I say, trying to keep the cringe out of my voice and off my face. I turn and walk around him, intent on heading to my room to throw a good sized pity party, but he grabs my upper arm. His eyes connect with mine and there is a lot written in them—nothing I want to decipher right now. I look away and shake my head. I whisper, "I can't." He drops my arm like I burned him and I walk away without looking back.

Once In my room, I close the door and collapse onto the bed face first. I grasp the pillow and press it tightly to my mouth before screaming.

CHAPTER 10

Shaw

I stand in my living room as I listen to her faint scream. "Fuck," I growl to myself, knowing I just screwed up big time. The chemistry between us is enough to keep us warm in this blizzard.

The way she makes my heart beat faster in my chest and my mind scatter, barely able to contain a thought long enough to process it. I've never felt this for anyone, *ever*. This out of control.

I take a deep breath and breathe in her light floral scent. She's intoxicating. Her soft skin and her blue eyes that shine, even from behind the round frame of her glasses. The way she constantly pushes them up her nose in a nervous gesture. She's fucking adorable and I want her. I want her under me, but I also find that I want her around me. I want her here with me, and not in the forced, trapped kind of way, but instead I want her to want to be around me. I need to make it up to her. I need to prove to her that I'm sorry. She didn't want me to see, but I could tell I hurt her feelings by misjudging her character.

I can understand that. Being a Marine, loyalty and honor are important. I can see now that she has both. I want that loyalty. Heading over to the stairs, I make my way to my bedroom in the loft. In the bathroom, I remove my clothes and turn on the shower. I need to think of a way to make it up to her. I want her. I realize that now. I realize that meeting her at Ron's that night was kismet. It has to be. The feelings are growing right now at what seems like a rapid pace, but maybe they have been growing this whole time, only suppressed by my anger at her from her supposed betrayal. Once I had realized that none of this was her fault, that she was innocent. I could feel the anger deflate out of me like a pin in a balloon. I get in the shower and stand there under the warm stream as I try to calm and gather my scattered thoughts.

After my shower, I walk into my closet with the towel around my waist. I grab two t-shirts. I wish I would have thought to grab her bags. Her car is sitting on the side of the road with a hole in the window, and probably buried under a few feet of snow by now. I toss on the t-shirt along with a pair of boxers and sweats before I head back downstairs and down the hallway that leads to the spare room where Aleice is staying.

I knock with two quick taps before saying, "I brought you a fresh shirt, figured you could use it. Sorry I didn't think of it sooner." Well really, before I didn't care that she was wearing the same dirty clothes because she was a money-stealing, back-stabbing bitch. But I digress. I hear her shuffle over to the door and it opens just a crack. I see her fingers reach through. I smirk as I hand over the shirt through the small gap in the door.

"Thanks," she grumbles before closing the door again. The water for the shower kicks on before I even turn to leave.

Making my way back to the living room, I check our firewood. We have a decent amount stored up, but if we get stuck here for more than a few days, we could run out. Knowing what I need to do, I walk over to the door and grab my jacket off the hanger and slide my feet into my boots. I grab my hat and gloves, too. I'm sure I'll keep warm once I'm moving. The nor'easter is due to hit us within the next two days. For now, we just have the few feet that hit us originally.

I open the door and trudge through the

snow, making my way around the side toward the small shed. I've got a small workshop in there and it's where I store the extra wood that won't fit in the house. When I get there, I grab the ax. I need to find a dead tree. A live one won't burn well, and I won't have time to season it. With all the wood being wet, I need it to dry fast. There is more wood than I remember in the shed. That might just save our asses. I close the shed and head toward the woods in search of some hard, dead trees.

After walking for about ten minutes, I find an oak that's cracking at the base where the snow has reached. The tree is definitely dead, so I get to chopping. After about an hour and a half of breaking all the wood down into smaller chunks, I make trip after trip, carrying all the pieces back to the shed, where I cut them down into firewood. The process is slow going, and it's not proving to be a very good distraction. After a while my body kicks into autopilot and my brain focuses on a very sexy girl that is currently in my house in nothing but my t-shirt. I bite my lip as I stifle a groan that wants to work its way out of my mouth at the thought of those perfect, strong, smooth legs.

I try to clear my head and focus on the wood. I need this to keep us warm. But my mind always goes back to her. All day she's been in the back of my mind. I want to get to know this girl. I've never had the desire to even talk to a girl after a night with her. Aleice is different, she's smart and funny and doesn't seem to give two shits whether I have money or not. I've seen the way she walks around my cabin; yes, she is in awe of it, but it's more than that. She's comfortable here. She likes the simple things, too. Most girls see my penthouse and their eyes flicker with dollar signs, but not Aleice.

Bringing all the already-seasoned wood that was in the shed into the house, I see there is enough to last a week or two, but if we keep getting hit with snow, we'll be screwed. I put all the wood I just chopped into the shed to season. Before turning on the de-humidifier to help speed up the process, I use my moisture meter to test the moisture: 35%. The wood won't burn well until it's under 20%. Let's hope I can get it down in a week. I shake off the worry that we could freeze and head back toward the door. Leaving my boots just inside, I hang up my jacket and hat and remove my gloves. "Fuck." I shiver slightly as I make my way inside to sit next to the fire. While I was moving it didn't seem that bad, but man, is it cold!

I check the time. Quarter after two. I head to the kitchen to make myself some lunch. Opening the fridge, I see a sandwich wrapped in cling wrap. I smile to myself. Even when she hates me, she still takes care of me. I nod my head slightly. That says a lot about the kind of person she is.

I take the sandwich out of the fridge and

plop down at the island. Looking around, I see she made a BLT with the left-over bacon from the Frittata. I take a bite and groan. Damn, that's good. A man could get used to this—being in the only place that's ever felt truly like home, with an amazing woman who cooks. Now, if only I could get her to stop hating me. I roll my eyes at myself.

Once I finish eating, I wash my plate and take a seat on the couch. I glance over at my books, thinking of grabbing one and relaxing when I notice they are out of order. I stand and make my way over to the built-in bookcases lining the wall behind the couch. As I skim through, I see she must have read almost all my Tom Clancy books. I chuckle to myself; damn, poor girl must have been really bored. I grab one of my favorites by him, one I've already read a handful of times, and take it back to the couch with me.

CHAPTER 11

Aleice

After a nap, I wake to find it's dark outside. I did not mean to sleep that long. I run my hands down my face and yawn. Now I'll never be able to sleep tonight. I blow out a puff of air, frustrated with myself. Oh, well. Nothing I can do about it now.

I head to the kitchen to make us some dinner. I have to say that I honestly enjoy this domesticity. I always wanted a family and now that I'm getting older, my body seems too long for it even more—I just never thought I would get it. Working as much as I do doesn't exactly lend itself well to dating. Plus, most of the guys who like me end up being nerds—which is fine—but they see me as competition or a threat to their intelligence. They end up turning everything into a game of who's smarter, then get pissed when I win. I roll my eyes. The male ego is something I'm not sure I will ever truly understand.

As I dig through the cabinets, I find a ton of pasta and canned goods, which makes sense—it lasts long and stores easy. I grab the spaghetti with a can of diced tomatoes from one cabinet and get basil and garlic from another for spaghetti with tomato basil sauce. Something simple, but delicious. I boil the water for the pasta and while that's going; I get out another pan and sauté the garlic slightly, then add the tomatoes. Instantly, the house smells like Italian cuisine. I smile to myself.

I feel arms wrap around me from behind, slowly caressing my hips before moving to my belly and pulling me firmly back into a muscular chest. A small gasp leaves my mouth as I feel his hands. How the hell did he sneak up on me? The dude has got to be 250 pounds of pure muscle.

While I'm debating this, he leans down, and I feel his warm breath slide across my cheek as he whispers in my ear, "I could get used to this. You're spoiling me." I smirk slightly, despite myself as he nibbles on my ear. I shiver at the contact. I hear him chuckle behind me. Before I can chastise him for touching me, he's already letting me go. I let go a breath I didn't realize I was holding.

I spin so that I'm facing him. "I enjoy cooking. Just be thankful you're able to be on the receiving end of it." The left side of my face rises as I playfully push him farther back. I turn back around so I can focus on the food, not wanting another frittata incident. "Have a seat. It should be ready shortly," I tell him as I glance over my shoulder to see he is still standing where I left him, eyes firmly on my ass. I shake my head but can't help but feel the confidence boost that having the attention of a man as sexy as he is brings.

Without a word, he rounds the island and sits down on the chair. "How long have you been cooking for?" he asks, and I pause for a second to contemplate that.

"Well, my mom used to love cooking, and she taught me everything I know... she started teaching me around age seven." I laugh to myself as I think about it. "She always used to say 'Aleice, the way to a man's heart is through his stomach, You want a good man? You better be able to cook good food.'" I smile as I think of her; it still hurts but I try to keep the wonderful memories of her alive, a way of keeping her in my heart so she's always close.

I glance over at him as I feel the slight sting at the back of my eyes. I won't cry right now. I take a deep breath and smile again when he says, "She must have been an amazing woman."

I bite the inside of my cheek to starve off the tears that want to fall. "She was the best."

He nods and a soft smile plays on his lips. We go silent after that; he must sense that I need a minute to get myself back together.

I drain the water and mix the sauce in with the pasta before plating them and grating some parmesan cheese over the top. When I turn around to put his plate down, he's gone. I glance around to see where he may have gone, but I see nothing. My brows furrow in confusion.

A moment later, he returns with a bottle of white wine and my smile returns. This man is speaking my language.

"Where've you been hiding that?" I say, eyeing the bottle.

"That's for me to know and you not to find out." He chuckles as he opens a drawer in the kitchen and takes out a bottle opener. Popping the cork, he grabs two wine glasses before pouring them.

"Now the meal's complete," I say as I take my glass over to my seat.

"Hmm," he grunts in agreement before joining me.

I watch as he takes his first generous bite. His eyes slide closed as he groans in approval. When he's finally done chewing, he says, "Oh, yeah. Your mom was right!"

I chuckle, happy that he's enjoying my food. I take a bite and have to admit it is pretty damn good.

Two hours later, and two bottles of wine down, I'm feeling good. I'm in that light zone, where everything feels good, and I don't give two fucks. We are laughing, and the conversation just flows so easily, it reminds me of the night we met. The attraction is still there. I mean, how can it not be with a man as gorgeous as Shaw. His hair is slicked back from him running his hands through it, and the silver at his temples reminds me of his maturity, of how different he is than the boys that I'm normally around. His full soft lips that he keeps licking so much they are turning pink. His eyes raking over my body like I'm a gallon of water in the desert. He lies back on the couch and his knees spread wide, his arms stretching behind his head. I can't help but glance down and notice the large bulge in his pants. My eyes shoot back to his face, and I see his smirk and his eyes light up, He achieved his goal. He moves his right hand out from behind his head and strokes himself back and forth from root to tip over his sweatpants. I bite my lip as I remember how good that cock felt inside me. I clear my throat and slide my glasses back up my face, knowing that I look flushed with desire. A part of me knows I can't let this happen. He had me fired and could have cost me my credibility, but the other part of me is dying to feel the pleasure that only he has given me.

He uses his other hand to summon me closer. My body follows his unspoken command without permission.

"Kneel," he states, the command clear is his tone. My legs buckle and I drop to my knees. He groans when he sees me following in his direction. "You enjoy following my commands, don't you? You want to be dominated. Your body craves it."

I sit in silence, not sure what to say. My body heats in response, clearly knowing something I don't.

"Answer me," he growls as he grabs my face, forcing me to look at him.

"Yes," I whimper as his hand glides down to wrap around my throat.

"Say it," he says as his fingers tighten slightly.

I stare into his eyes, silently asking him if he was saying what I think he's saying. He gives me a slight nod, confirming my suspicions. "Daddy…" I whisper, still not believing that's what he wants.

His eyes close as if absorbing my words.

"That's right, baby girl, I'm your daddy and you want your daddy to feel good, don't you?" I nod my head vehemently, so turned on I can feel my core pulsing beneath my borrowed shirt.

"Good girl, now take daddy's thick cock out of his pants." He lets go of my throat and rests his hands on his large, muscular thighs. My hands reach for his sweats, pulling at the waistband to pull them down as he lifts his hips to help me. I pull them all the way down to his ankles, where he takes them off and moves them aside. He sits in front of me in all his masculine glory, his boxer briefs tented enough to protect a small family from the rain. I'm practically drooling at the thought of getting him in my mouth.

"You want it?" he growls out, and I nod again. His cocky smirk lights up my already blown out pupils. "Then take it, baby."

I eagerly reach for his briefs and pull them down as well, completely freeing his enormous cock as it springs up and hits his belly button. My eyes widen as I take in the sight. How could I possibly forget how large he is? His beautiful cock stands thick and proud. I grab it at the base before licking my way up to the tip, where I lick up the pre-cum that is dripping there. I look up at him and see him staring straight at me. Seeing the look on his face gives me the confidence I need to take him into my mouth. Swirling my tongue around the tip before taking him to the back of my throat. God, he tastes so good. We moan simultaneously.

"That's it, such a good fucking girl, give daddy want he needs. Watching you walk around my house in my clothes. Those sexy legs I can't stop picturing wrapped around my face." I moan again at his dirty words. Why is that so sexy? I feel myself soaking through my panties. I pull back until it's just the tip that's in my mouth, taking a large breath and opening my throat as I work my way back down so that he is all the way at the back. He moans as I swallow around his cock, and he barriers himself deep in my throat. My eyes water as I gag.

"That's right baby, gag on this big cock."

I pull back and moan

again as I catch my breath. I lift his shaft, licking the underside before sucking the tip into my mouth and hollowing out my cheeks.

"Fuck yes baby girl, that feels so good." His head tilts back as he rests it on the back of the couch.

Before I have time to process what's going on, he stands and lifts me under my butt, placing me on my back on the couch. He reaches behind his neck and pulls his shirt off over his head. He lifts the hem of my shirt and pulls it over my head.

Leaning back to look at me fully, he shakes his head and I try to fight the urge to cover myself, but lose when my hands snake over my large breasts. I've never been self-conscious of my body, but it's hard not to be when someone is staring at you the way he is staring at me.

He catches my hands in his and says, "No!" He shakes his head again. "You have the most amazing body I've ever seen. You are drop dead gorgeous and I hardly feel worthy to look at this perfection."

I feel my eyes widen in shock and my cheeks redden at his affirmation. I run my hands down his chest to his abs. Feeling bold, I say, "When you first sat down next to me at the bar, I thought, how is this man possible? You are by far the sexiest man I've ever seen," I say, awe clear in my voice.

He smirks as he moves his mouth to mine, taking my lips in his, gently sliding his tongue into my mouth. I swear I see stars. How is it that someone can blow my mind with just a kiss? I slowly lift my pelvis and rock myself against his erection. I moan at the contact. His lips leave mine and he works his way down my neck and over my collarbone. "You taste divine." He says as he continues to work his way down my body. He reaches for my panties, before slowly sliding them down my thighs all the way to my feet so I can kick them off. He sucks my nipple into his mouth, swirling it around before sucking it firmly. I gasp, then whimper at the sensation.

"So... good," I pant as his other hand works over my other breast before pinching my nipple. He works his way across my chest before taking the other nipple into his mouth and repeating the action. I run my fingers down his back, letting my nails rake over his skin before working my way back up and dragging my hands through his hair before tugging slightly. He groans and nips my breast before kissing and licking his way down my flat stomach. Stopping before he gets where I need him, I raise my hips to encourage him further. He smirks and runs his hands down my ribs before tracing them over the curves of my hips, and wrapping them under my thighs.

"It's time I finally see these amazing legs wrapped around my face." He barely gets the last word out before he buries his face in my pussy. He curses as he licks me up from my opening all the way to my clit and back, only stopping once to swirl his tongue inside me. "Just as sweet as I remember," he says right against my clit.

The vibration drives me wild. "Yes... daddy," I say tentatively.

"That's right, baby. I'm your daddy."

I groan at his words. Fuck, why do I love that so much? He works my clit with teasing licks and alternating soft and hard suction until my legs are shaking and I'm having a hard time catching my breath. "Oh, god!" I feel my orgasm rising faster and faster. He must sense that I'm close because he slams his fingers inside me and sucks hard on my clit and my vision blacks. I hear myself screaming his name but can barely register when it started or how the words are leaving my mouth. He continues to lick me lightly as I slowly come back down.

He works his way back up my body before kissing my lips and making me taste myself. He sucks my bottom lip into his mouth before nipping it and letting it go with a pop. He stares into my eyes. "So beautiful," he says as his hard cock nudges my opening before rubbing back and forth over my sensitive clit. I shiver at the over-stimulation before he slides all the way in, with one firm thrust. Once he's in, he stills and moans.

"Fuck, this pussy feels so goddamn good, squeezing me so tight. I'm going to make you soak daddy's cock." He pulls back and slowly works his way back in. His pace is maddeningly slow. I lift my hips to meet his thrusts. His pelvis rubs my clit with each pump. I moan his name again and again.

"Your cock feels so good inside me. So full!" I murmur as I scrape my nails down his back before squeezing his ass in my hands. I close my eyes as I focus on how good it all feels. To be in his arms again, to have this amazing man's attention, is a powerful feeling.

I open my eyes and I see he's staring right at me. He shifts his weight onto one hand so he can use his right hand to caress my face. He looks like he is looking right into my soul. It's unnerving. This is just sex. I can't give this man my heart when they are no chance in hell that he would give me his in return. I try to look away, but he holds my head still by sliding his hand under my chin to cup my head.

"Stay with me, baby," he says when he sees me trying to turn away. His eyes bounce back and forth from mine before he leans in and kisses me.

There is so much passion, I'm blown away. His hungry mouth searches for more, so I slide my tongue against his. He groans and pumps his hips faster. His right hand pulls off my chin and goes to the couch next to my head while his other hand goes under my butt to lift me up to the angle he wants.

"Oh, God!" I pant as he hits that deep G-spot repeatedly.

"Yes, sweetheart. Feel me deep inside this perfect little pussy."

It feels so good I can hardly focus, my orgasm building and building. Wanting to take him with me, I clench down on him, squeezing as tight as I can. He grunts like someone has punched him in the gut.

"Fuck," he growls out as his hips piston into me, hard and fast.

"You want my come baby? To fill this tight little pussy so full it leaks out of you?" he groans in my ear.

I scream as I come, not able to hold on after hearing those words. My body stiffens as my legs shake and my body trembles. My eyes close automatically, not able to handle the onslaught of pleasure coursing through my body. After the second clench, I hear him shout my name as he comes with me. I feel his cock jerking inside me as he fills me with his seed. He slows his strokes but continues to slide in and out to prolong the pleasure for us both.

He collapses, half on me, half on the inside of the couch next to me, and I enjoy his warmth and the comforting weight he's putting on me. Turning my head to face him, I see he has a huge smile on his face and his eyes are closed. I chuckle to myself. I did that. If that isn't an ego boost, I'm not sure what is.

"Is it just me, or does it seem to get better every time?" I whisper to him.

His eyes pop open, and his smile turns into a smug grin. "Oh, baby. Those weren't even my best moves. It'll just keep getting better from here." He winks and I laugh.

CHAPTER 12

Shaw

After I've got my bearings back, I stand and walk over to the kitchen for a few paper towels. I wet them and bring them back to clean her up.

"Thank God for leather couches," I smirk as I wipe the leather clean. She chuckles and puts the shirt I was wearing over her head. I smile, liking her in my clothes. Once partially dressed again, she grabs the front of the shirt and brings it up to her nose for a deep sniff. She lets out a little moan.

"You smell so good," she shivers, thoroughly enjoying my scent. I pick up the one she was wearing; I throw that one and do the same. She sees me and her eyes shine happily as she watches. It smells like her—flowery like shampoo but with a natural sweetness to it that feels comforting. Her scent is comfort and warmth. I drop it and head over to the kitchen again.

"Hungry?" I ask her, almost as if responding to the question as her stomach grows.

"Just a little snack. We need to be mindful of how much we eat. We don't know how long we will be stuck here," she says, waving her hands around to encompass all the snow.

"Good point," I concede and pull out some canned peanuts to snack on. "This all right?" I hold them up and she nods. I also grab us both a glass of water.

"So, Shaw Hutchens, what made you want to start a security company?" she asks, her eyes looking up and me with curiosity.

"Well, I joined the Marines at age eighteen and after every tour, I would come back home and feel lost. I didn't have any trade skills or a college degree. So, I would go back and do it all again. After six tours, I was no longer fit for duty since I was getting older, and I fucked up my knee on my last mission. I was fortunate enough not to have too much PTSD. I have some triggers, but nothing that affects my day-to-day. Me and Reed had been bull shittin' one night after having a few too many and he mentioned security, how it would be a great fit for us, but he didn't know how we would be able to find a job in it. And that's where the concept came from. So, when I got back from duty, I got to work on how to start a business and I knew right away I wanted to hire other veterans. With a veteran unemployment rate of five and a half percent, I felt I needed to do something to help them out. Reed was actually the one who suggested we venture into cyber security, too." I finally look back at her after talking animatedly with my hands. I clench my fists at my sides.

She smiles as she says, "It's great to see you are so passionate about this. I can feel how much it means to you." She reaches out and runs her hand down my arm before squeezing her hand over my fist. "It's an amazing thing, what you're doing for those veterans." She smiles again and let's go of my fist.

"What about you? How'd you get into computers?" I ask, eager to learn more about this brilliant woman.

She chuckles. "Well, I really like puzzles." I look at her with a look of pure confusion. "Hacking is how I got started," she clarifies. "Coding and programming are like gigantic puzzles where you have to find just the right piece to go in, just the right spot or you won't be able to complete the puzzle. I love the challenge, too. I kind of just wandered into hacking and from that, the curiosity grew, I just had to keep going, keep learning and pushing myself until I mastered it. I would stay up all hours of the night hacking and coding and pushing myself to get better." She shrugs as if it's nothing.

"And how did you figure out you could hack into government facilities?" I ask, recalling how she told me she could do it when she was hacking into our network at Hutchens & Co.

"Ah… the less you know about that, the better." She snorts and quickly looks away, pushing her glasses back up her nose.

I nod. She's probably right. "So, seeing as I already called Reed to let him know Jace is not only fired but we have evidence that he was the one who stole the clients' money and was hacking into their accounts, I would like to ask you to work for me again. To be the head of my Cyber Security department. Under Reed, of course," I quickly add.

She raises her eyebrow and purses her lips to the side, and she ponders the idea.

"I'll give you a big raise on top of what I'm already going to pay you for your new hack-proof firewall program," I say to sweeten the deal. Needing this girl, not only at my company but also with me. This connection between us, it's not just sexual, although that connection is growing exponentially the longer we are around each other. But the feelings I'm having for this girl go beyond anything I've ever felt for anyone before. I want more of it. *I want more of her.*

When she doesn't respond, I know I need more. "Look..." I grab her hands and hold them in mine while I look her in the eyes so she can see how much I mean what I'm about to say. "I'm so sorry, I shouldn't have blamed you or jumped so quickly into thinking you would have done that to me. It's just hard not to protect the company I've spent so much time making. That's not only my livelihood but the livelihood of all the men that are on my team. I didn't know you then like I do now."

She nods her head and I know she understands. "I understand. I'll do it," she says as a smile lights up her beautiful face. I take her in again. Her slightly rounded face with a smattering of light freckles across her nose and cheeks. Her round glasses that cover a quarter of her gorgeous face, from her high cheekbones to her eyebrows. I look at her full bottom lip as she bites the inside.

I quickly close the distance between us pulling her against me and wind my arms around her back before I take her lips in mine. There's a slight twinge of electricity as our lips connect, like when you're a kid and you rub your socks back and forth against the carpet. I take that juicy bottom lip between my lips, sucking lightly, before running my tongue along the edge of it. I wonder how I came to care about her so much in such a short amount of time. I haven't known her long, but with everything being so natural between us, it feels like I've known her so much longer. I rub my hands up and down her back before taking my left hand up into her hair to clench it in my fist.

She lets out a little puff of air as her head tilts back into my hand. I pull her left leg up to wrap it around me. "You're insatiable," she smirks against my lips.

"Only for you," I say as I take back her mouth. I pick up her other leg and she hops slightly so that they wrap completely around me. My hands go to her round ass as I carry her up the stairs to my loft. I carry her over to the bed, laying her down before breaking the kiss.

"We don't have to do anything if you don't want. We can just snuggle." I smirk, knowing that she's as wound up as I am.

"Of course we can," she says as she rocks her hips against my growing erection. "Why don't you snuggle inside me," she giggles as she says it, and I can't help but laugh with her. I nuzzle my face against the crook of her neck, breathing her in. I pull my sweats down and push her shirt up over her hips, gliding my hands up and down her sexy curves. I grab my stiff cock and rub it around her clit. Circling the tip around and around the tight little nub. She mewls and pants as she rocks her hips faster to get more constant pressure.

I tsk her as she tries to top from bottom. "I'm in control, baby girl, *always*." She bites her lip so hard it turns white.

"Yesss…" she groans through her teeth.

"That's what you needed, isn't it sweetheart? A man. You needed *me. Only me*." I use my cock to rub her faster and more firmly, putting direct pressure just above her clit, and she explodes for me. "That's it, baby. It's my big cock that makes you come that hard." I lower my cock and force my way inside her clenching core while my fingers gently stroke her clit to keep her orgasm going.

"God, yes, Shaw!"

Hearing her say my name drives me mad. I grab her hips and pound into her, hard and fast. The raw brutality I'm using as I grind myself against her is purely animalistic. She chants 'yes' as I bottom out in her tight little cunt.

"That's it baby, come again for me," I growl as I rub my fingers against her nub again before pinching it lightly.

"Ahh," she yells as she comes on my cock. Losing all control, I close my eyes as I drill into her. Once she's coming back down, I pull out and flip her onto her stomach before slapping my hand against her ass once, twice, three times. She yelps, but pushes her hips back against my hand. I smooth my hands over the red mark I left on her ass. Grabbing my shaft, I line myself up and slowly slide myself home again. I reach around and slide my fingers through her folds, getting them nice and wet before I remove my hand. She makes a small whining noise until she feels my fingers sliding over her back entrance, rubbing small circles while applying light pressure.

"Oh, oh," she moans as she enjoys my ministrations.

I slowly slide one finger into her hole, and I feel her tighten up.

"Relax baby, I won't hurt you." I say, as I work my finger in and out of her tight ring.

"I've never had anyone back there before…" she says, nerves clear in her voice.

"Like I said, baby, you needed me." I wink as she glances back at me over her shoulder.

She giggles slightly before dropping her forehead to the mattress. I hear her mumble, "maybe I did."

I rut into her after that to prove that she did. Just as much as I needed her. I feel the tingles as they work their way up my spine, and my balls tighten, preparing to dump my load deep inside her womb. The thought makes something primal in me clench and I come with a groan, holding myself as deep as I can as I empty myself inside her. "Aleice," I cry as I do. She reaches down and rubs herself while I finish, and she finishes shortly after. I pull her to the side, still buried inside her. I pull her into me and cover us with the blanket.

Rubbing my nose over the back of her head through her long brown hair, I breathe her in. She smells so good. I kiss the crown of her head twice before moving my hand up to hold her breast under the shirt, still buried inside her as my cock remains half hard. I hear her make a little contented noise as she gets comfortable. Not long after, her breathing evens out and my eyes get heavy as I listen to the soothing sound of her soft snores.

The next few days, as the snow piles up outside, we stay warm in a cocoon of each other. She's pretty much constantly wrapped in my arms, and I don't want to let her go.

CHAPTER 13

Aleice

I've forgiven him, somewhere between the sex and time spent talking, getting to know each other better. I know he did what he did to protect his guys, the people that depend on him. He didn't know me at the time, so I can't blame him for jumping to conclusions, even if it hurt.

These last few days have been so blissfully normal. Days filled with waking up in Shaw's arms or with his tongue between my legs—his preferred way to wake me up. I make us breakfast and lunch, then we make dinner together. We sit and talk, or we read next to each other on the couch, or we play a few games of cards.

"Royal flush," I smirk as I drop my cards in front of me.

His eyes widen slightly before he drops his cards face down. "I'm going to go broke before we get out of this snow," he chuckles, shocked at the outcome.

"We could always switch to strip poker," I tease as I rake my eyes down his glorious chest and bite my lip.

He gets that smug look on his face that he always gets when I check him out—which is a lot. He slides his chair back and pats his lap. I make my way slowly around the island till I sit down on his lap. My hand strokes over his now-full beard. I think I like it even better. He closes his eyes and groans as I scratch across his scruff. I giggle. Then, while his eyes are still closed, I sneak a kiss to his lips. Before I have time to pull back, he grabs me and pulls me in for a proper kiss, licking my bottom lip until I open for his tongue.

"What am I going to do with you?" I question as I pull away from his lips, a smirk marring my face.

"Oh, I can think of a few things you can do with me," he states, as his hands slide down to my backside before squeezing it tightly in his hands.

"You old perv," I say as I giggle and push my hands against his chest to stand.

"Don't I know it," he replies with a smirk and a wink before standing and letting me slide all the way down his body. I moan as I enjoy the feel on his hard muscles scraping against my soft body.

I take a deep breath, trying not to think about the future and what it might hold. I can't help but be falling for Shaw. I mean, I'm spending 24/7 with the guy, it was bound to happen with all the attraction and chemistry between us. I tried —I really did—to keep up the wall, but in the end, it crumbled like dried out papier mâché. And I can honestly say I'm happy about it. I haven't been this happy in a long time. It feels like I have met the other half of me, the opposite, but also the same in many ways. Complimentary. But what if the feelings that I'm sensing from him are only because we are trapped here together? What if, once we are free again, things go back to the way they were? Will he still want to be with me? Fuck, is he even with me? Gahhh...

I shake my head to clear my thoughts. The snow stopped a few hours ago but now we are left with a good five feet of snow from the two snow-falls; luckily, we didn't get as much as anticipated. I glance out the front wall of windows and see the trees painted white, with heavy drifts of snow covering all the branches. Looks like something from an old Bob Ross painting.

Speaking of old, "Fuck," all but bursts out of me as the thought hits my head.

"What? What's wrong?" he says, concern lacing his tone.

"I need your phone. I've been so caught up here with you, I never thought about calling my roommate or my dad. They probably think I'm lying in a ditch somewhere. Oh my God, I'm a horrible person." I pace back and forth, rubbing my hands together before wiping my sweaty palms on my shirt. Shaw reaches out and grabs both my shoulders to steady me.

"It's okay, just call them now and let them know you're okay." He walks over to the coffee table to grab his phone. "The service here is pretty spotty, so it doesn't always work," he says will a frown as he hands it over to me.

Thank God I memorized my dad's number, at least. Quickly dialing, I listen for it to connect.

"Hello?" Dad answers on the third ring, agitation and worry in his voice.

"Dad!" I say to let him know it's me calling from the unknown number.

He lets out an audible sigh of relief. "Jesus Pete, Aleice. I've been worried sick about you.

Where the hell have you been? I've been calling your phone since Christmas day!" The anger is back.

"I know, dad. I'm so sorry... On the way up the mountain, my car slid on some black ice and I hit a tree, the car's probably totaled. But luckily..." I pause, trying to think of how to describe Shaw on the fly, "a friend from work was going up to his cabin and rescued me. But we have been snowed in ever since. All my stuff was left in the car," I explain.

I can still hear the anger in his voice, but he seems to be relaxing just a bit. "Okay, where are you?" I look at Shaw, who is standing right next to me, clearly able to hear both sides of the conversation.

"A little over six clicks east of Deerborn Road," he tells me. I furrow my brow.

What the fuck is a click? "Ugh... Did you hear that, dad?" I ask, so I don't have to relay the message.

"Yeah, I heard it." His voice seems to be angrier now, although I'm not sure why. "How much snow did y'all get up there?" he asks with all his southern charm. Dad was born and raised in Georgia, and there is something so comforting about his twang. I didn't realize how much I had missed it until this moment.

"Ugh, my guess based on just looking at it, probably close to five feet." I cringe as I tell him.

"Oh, for the love of Pete."

I can almost hear him running his hand down his face in frustration. He takes a deep breath before blowing it out directly into the phone's speaker, causing it to crackle. I wince and pull the phone away from my ear before returning it.

"Okay, I'll call the tow company and have them bring it back to a shop by the condo," he says as he's putting together all the necessary steps to make this right.

Shaw speaks up then. "No need. I already took care of it. I had it sent to my shop. They got it a few nights ago before the second storm. They will look at it as soon as they get a chance and send me a report on it shortly after." A small grin lines Shaw's mouth as he tells me this.

My eyes widen and my jaw drops.

He whispers just for me to hear, "I got you, baby girl." His hand slides down my back, not in a sexual way, but it still lights up all the nerves in my body just the same.

I shiver slightly at his touch before I smile. I mouth back, "Thank you." He just nods.

"Alright, well, I'm glad that's taken care of. Now, how do I get you out?"

I can hear the begrudging respect in my dad's voice at what Shaw had said about my car.

"Not entirely sure how you can unless you got the plow," I joke.

"Hmm," dad grunts, like it's not a half bad idea.

"I'm all right, I'm safe and warm and have plenty of food. I'm good," I say as I reach up and rub the spot on my forehead that still has a slight cut on it.

"Yeah, well, I don't like it," he huffs, and I can't help but chuckle.

"Dad, I'm 28 years old. I'm not a nun. I can be around men," I say, using my hand to stifle the giggle that's rising in my throat and threatening to break loose.

"Oh, darlin', I don't need to hear that. In my head you're the virgin Mary."

The laugh I was barely containing burst through. I even hear dad chuckle with me.

"Oh, stop it. Let me keep my dream, all right," he huffs before quickly changing the subject. "Have you called Jamie yet? She's been calling my phone and even stopped by a few times to see if you were here."

"Nope, I called you first. I'll call her right now though. Would you mind giving me her number? I can't remember it off the top of my head," I ask before wandering into the kitchen for a piece of paper and a pen to write it down.

"Sure, hold on. Let me just go through my calls." I hear him pull the phone away, then some muffled grunts as he tries to figure out how to get to his recent calls.

I roll my eyes, thinking that I'm going to be waiting a while. "Do you need help, dad?" I ask politely after a few more grunts and low curses.

"No," he sulks, too stubborn to let me help him.

My head rolls back on my neck so I can stare at the ceiling. "You have to swipe up with your finger to go to the home screen. From there you hit the little phone icon on the bottom left hand corner of your phone." I try to speak slowly, as if I'm explaining the alphabet to a toddler.

"I said, I got it," he grunts, but I hear him mumble, 'oh, there is it' softly in the background. I smile and shake my head to myself. As he rattles off the number, I write it down.

"Thank you. I love you and I'll keep in

touch, okay?" I tell him before we disconnect.

"Okay, you do that. Love you, bug."

I smile at the nickname. Once the call has ended, Shaw says, "Bug?"

I smile again. "Yeah, he calls me his sugar-bug. Got a problem with that?" I say, raising an eyebrow at him.

"Nope, none at all," he says, raising his hands in mock surrender.

I nod. "We are going to have to get out of here at some point. We are already running low on food." I point in the direction of the kitchen.

He nods. "Yeah, I know. My truck has four-wheel drive, and I can load down the back with the cement blocks, but I'll need to clear a path somehow." He rubs his bearded chin with his thumb and forefinger. His eyes widen as if he just remembered something. Right as he is about to speak, the lights blink a few times before going off completely.

"Fuck!" he growls. "The power's out," he says, grabbing me and moving me clumsily over to the couch before pushing me down to my butt. "Stay here. I'll go grab some candles, and I think I have a lantern or two in the shed outside."

"And how are you going to get those?

Swim?" I chuckle at the thought of him doing the backstroke in the snow.

He snickers with me. "If I have to," he responds as he walks away and feels his way around the house to get the candles. He carries four of them over to the living room and puts them down on the coffee table. "It's going to smell like a Yankee Candle asshole in here." He grunts as he lights the wick. I burst out laughing.

Reaching out, I grab his hand and haul him down onto the couch with me, then crawl into his lap and rest my head on his chest by his shoulder. Rubbing my face on him like a feral cat, I snuggle in. He chuckles and rubs my hair before kissing my forehead.

"Comfy?" he asks once I'm settled.

"Yep," I say, popping the 'p'. I feel his smirk against the top of my head.

CHAPTER 14

Shaw

I grab the blanket off the back of the couch and cover us both with it. I breathe in deep, soaking in her smell that seems to settle something deep in my chest. I try not to focus too hard on that. I harden at the smell of her and the feel of her bare pussy over my jeans. She finally gave up wearing panties when they just kept getting in the way of us being together. Plus, I think she got tired of washing them every day. As if sensing where my mind was wandering, she slowly grinds her core against my lap. My half chub quickly becomes rock-hard for her.

"What are you doing to me..." I whisper in her ear as I wrap her hair around my fist and pull her head back to make eye contact with her. I love her eyes. They are so open and seem to say a thousand things. A beautiful shade of blue that lightens when she's happy. She quickly sticks her tongue out and playfully licks my cheek. I can't help but smirk. This girl is funny, playful, smart, and gorgeous. She's everything I could have dreamed of.

I raise an eyebrow, my smirk remaining on my face. Then I count..."One... two... three..."

She gives me a curious look, before her eyes widen and she hops off me to go hide. I chuckle and continue to count.

"Four... five... six... seven..."

I hear her stumble and hit a few things, a soft grunt of "fuck" as she scurries around, trying to find a good hiding place. "Eight... nine... ten... eleven... twelve... thirteen... fourteen... fifteen... ready or not..."

I slowly stand, trying to be as quiet as possible. I grab a candle off the table and use it to light my way. I check behind the island and the wall that separates the hallway from the kitchen. I walk down to the room where she was staying and didn't see her there either. I check the office where I see the red light on, on my computer. What the fuck? I walk closer and see it's the camera. Without making it obvious that I see the camera on, I slowly back out of the room, closing the door behind me.

God damnit. Jace is watching us. I don't like this one bit.

I make my way back to the living room and up the spiral stairs to my loft. Sneaking my way into the bedroom, I find her lying on the bed under the covers like she's hiding from a monster. I guess she kind of is, isn't she? I place the candle down on the dresser and lower my hands so they are over her stomach, grabbing her fast. She screams as I tickle her. She thrashes around, laughing so hard I see tears streaming down her face. Her infectious laugh causes me to laugh, too. I make my way onto the bed and straddle her body as she continues to squirm under me.

I stop long enough for her to catch her breath. Her body slumps against the bed as she gulps down lungfuls of air. I settle back on my heels and watch her. My God, she the most breathtaking thing I've ever seen. In a flash, her arm rushes up and latches on to my nipple before twisting.

"Fuck," I grunt as she tosses her head back in a laugh. "That fuckin' hurt!" I growl out. But she's too busy laughing to acknowledge me. I move so I'm sitting at the head of the bed with my back against the headboard. She rolls onto her stomach to look at me. She has a playful smile on her face.

I enjoy seeing her smile. There's an itching sensation rising in my chest. I like putting that smile on her face. I like being the reason she's smiling. How is it this woman can come into my life and yet feel like she's always been here? There is no awkwardness or uncomfortable silence. I've never felt so... content. The good content, not the complacent content where everything in your life has been so stagnant that you just go about your routine. You get comfortable with the mundane because it could be worse. No, I'm actually happy. I haven't smiled or laughed or even really taken the time to enjoy life since I started my company, my focus solely on it the entire time.

I pat my lap, implying I would like her to rest her head there. Understanding without words, she moves up the bed and rests her head in my lap. I run my fingers through her hair, removing the tangles that I made while tickling her. She lets out a happy sigh as she takes my phone and continues to text with Jamie.

"When I was looking for you just now, I checked in the office and noticed the red light for the computer camera was on. Probably the mic, too," I tell her while continuing to slide my fingers over her scalp.

She stills. "Well, at least we haven't spent much time in there, so he couldn't have heard much," she says as if she's trying to convince herself more than me.

"Yeah. You're safe here with me, you know? I won't let anything happen to you." I run my thumb over her eyebrow and down her temple before tracing her cheekbone and jawline. She turns and her glasses go crooked on her face as the ear piece hits my leg. Quickly, she readjusts her head, so the glasses correct themselves before using her finger in that adorable way to push them up her little nose. She gets a pensive expression as her left hand trails down the center of my chest.

"I know... it's just, we can't stay here forever. Once we leave, he'll go right back to following me." She frowns, unease in her voice.

"Well, he would be dumb to do that because there is a warrant out for his arrest, and I'm sure I could spare one of my guys to watch you when you're not at work." I catch her hand before it slips further down again and bring it to my lips to kiss her palm. "Being your daddy means I take care of you... in all ways." I smirk and wink as she blushes and giggles.

"You're serious about that. I kinda' thought it was just a sex thing." Her face reddens further, and I chuckle. How can she still be shy after all the ways I've fucked her?

I shake my head. "It started out that way... but I don't know. I guess I kind of like the idea of being a daddy." I pause when I realize what I just said. The thought of kids has never crossed my mind. I was always too busy, or I was on tour. Now that the company is stable, and I have an amazing woman that I could see spending the rest of my life with, a family doesn't sound all that unattainable. But would she want that? As I stare at her, I don't see fear in her eyes. In fact, if I'm judging correctly, I see hope. I lift her under her shoulders and knees and scoop her until she's resting on my lap, cradled in my arms. Her head finds my neck, and she nuzzles in, taking deep breaths of my cologne.

"God, it smells so good," she mutters to herself, barely audible.

"I'll keep you safe," I reiterate, kissing her forehead and the top of her head.

She sighs, "I know," while wrapping her arm around my neck and into the back of my hair before she runs her fingers through it. Before long, she drifts off to sleep. The only sound in the room are her soft snores and steady breathing.

I close my eyes and relax as I hold her to my chest. A feeling of calm settles over me. Everything's perfect.

CHAPTER 15

Aleice

I wake with a start to the sound of banging. When I finally catch my breath after having it literally scared out of me, I notice I'm alone in bed and it's still dark—which doesn't means much since the power is out. I throw off the covers that Shaw must have tucked me under at some point and make my way to the balcony of the loft, looking down on the living area and the front door. I see Shaw standing there wielding an ax as he goes to open the door. Now that I'm out of the room, I see that it's actually light out, but just barely; I would guess it's five or six in the morning. The banging continues and

Shaw grabs the handle and throws the door open. I see my dad standing there in the open doorway.

"Dad!" I yell, startling both men.

Shaw lowers his ax and takes a step back. Dad takes the opportunity to step inside and close the door behind him. I tuck the shirt close to my legs so I don't reveal anything while racing down the spiral stairs. Once I get there, I throw my arms around Dad's neck, and he quickly squeezes me into his chest.

"I'm so glad you're safe, bug," he says with relief in his voice.

"Of course, I told you I was. What wasn't safe is you traveling all the way here in this weather! How on earth did you get here, anyway?" I sink back to flat feet and hold him at arm's length.

"I put the plow on," he replies while taking a step back and glaring at Shaw.

"Ahh..." I nod my head in understanding. Dad has a plow that he uses to do all the local businesses'—including the diner—parking lots. He says it gives him something to do and they slip him some money under the table. It's cheap and they don't have to wait for the state plows to do it.

When he's done sizing up Shaw, he turns his attention back to me and notices all I'm wearing is a t-shirt. Yikes, this is awkward.

"Made yourself comfortable, I see," he says in a disapproving tone, and I shrink into myself a little.

"Dad, this is Shaw, he rescued me after I got into the wreck and was knocked unconscious," I say, hoping to get the focus off me, if only temporarily.

He glances at Shaw again before taking in what I said. His head whips back to me. "Knocked unconscious!?" He glares at me.

Oops, I probably shouldn't have mentioned that part. I forgot I didn't bring that up on the phone. "Look, I'm fine, just a small cut. I smacked my head on the side window in the crash, but I'm fine. I swear." I hold my arms out to him to show him I'm all right. He still looks angry, but Shaw thankfully steps in.

"It's nice to meet you sir," he says, gesturing towards the couch. "Why don't we have a seat and Ally can go put her clothes on. She was just sleeping," he mentions, in way of clarification as to my clothes, pretending as though I haven't been like this all week.

I smile at him in gratitude and head toward the back bedroom. Luckily, I had washed all the clothes a few days prior. I quickly throw them all on and make my way back out of the kitchen. "Coffee?" I ask as I start the pot.

"Yes please," they both reply at the same time. I smile to myself, readying three cups, making them up just the way I know they like. When I bring the mugs over, dad, not being one to hold back, gets right into his interrogation.

"So, how old are you, Shaw?" he asks, and I choke and sputter on the sip that just hit my throat. I pound my fist into my chest to get myself together.

Shaw smirks and says, "I'm forty-three, sir."

I see dad doing the math in his head, not liking the number. "Fifteen years is a big difference, don't you think?"

Subtle, dad, really subtle. I bow my head in embarrassment. Sweet jeez, this is mortifying, and I have a feeling it's only downhill from here.

Shaw nods his head in understanding, "I think it can be, depending on the person, but if you're both mature and want the same thing, I think age is only a minor factor," he politely responds.

Want the same thing? As in sex? Because, although I love that, it's not all I want. I want more. *I want it all.* Looking away so Shaw can't see the disappointment on my face, I take a sip of coffee.

Dad nods and says, "You can call me John."

Shaw nods his head and smiles.

"What do you do for work, Shaw?" dad asks, diving deeper into uncomfortable territory.

"I own Hutchens & Co. We manage private and cyber security."

I glance over at him and smile. Dad looks at me, brows furrowing, his eyes asking me a question. I nod once. And his frown deepens.

"So, you are Aleice's boss," dad says, commenting rather than asking.

"Not directly, no. Reed is her boss. I am just the owner and CEO. I never had direct contact with her. Reed takes care of everything in his department," Shaw clarifies.

Dad purses his lips and gives Shaw the stink eye.

I glance around, looking for a new topic. "Anyone hungry?" I say, and cringe at the panic in my voice. Dad gives me a knowing look, but thankfully doesn't call me out on it. I make my way back to the kitchen and get out all the ingredients for pancakes.

I listen quietly as they exchange war stories. Dad seems to perk up at this. Any excuse to talk about his time in Vietnam. I roll my eyes, but Shaw listens intently and even laughs a few times. Well, at least they are bonding.

Grabbing the plates, I carry them over to the coffee table and place them all down.

"Thanks bug," dad says, barely pausing in his story to take a bite.

"Thanks babe," Shaw says, and my cheeks heat at the endearment.

"When we are done eating, you can grab anything you have here, and we are going," dad states like there is no other option. He's already decided, and I don't want to upset my dad further, nor do I stay for the bubble to burst. I have to go back to reality, and accept that this is just sex for him. He has no commitment to me and doesn't seem to even want one. Like he said, *as long as they want the same thing*.

I nod "Okay, sure." I take a bite of my pancake and chew in silence, making sure not to look at Shaw. The silence quickly becomes uncomfortable. I finish my food and bring my dad's and my empty plates to the sink to clean them. Shaw has barely touched his.

Dad stands and shakes Shaw's hand. "Thank you for helping my daughter," he says begrudgingly. I had nothing other than the clothes on my back here, so we turn and head for the door.

Not even sure what day it is, I say, "See you

at work tomorrow?" I look to Shaw and see there's a small frown creasing his face.

"Of course. I'll get in touch with Jessica and get everything sorted."

He nods once and I look to the ground before saying, "Thanks."

Dad opens the door, and we head out to his beat-up pickup truck with the plow on the front. I walk around and hop into the passenger's side, making sure not to look back at Shaw. It was just an escape, nothing more, both of us lost in the fantasy created by being alone in the wilderness with nothing but the two of us. We both just got caught up in it. I don't even know if he meant half the stuff he said. At least I have my job back. Dad and I remain silent as we slowly drive back to the main road.

"You like him," dad states, staring straight ahead, making sure not to look in my direction.

"It's complicated," I say, even though it wasn't a question. I'm not really sure what to say to that. I consider my options: Yeah, I do, but it's just sex? Yeah, I do, but as you so eloquently stated, he is fifteen years older than me and my boss? Yeah, I do, but he doesn't want me the way I want him? Oof. Yeah, let's just go with 'it's complicated'.

He shakes his head like he sees something I don't. "Let's just get you home."

I nod. Yeah, he's right. One thing at a time. We make idle chitchat as we make our way back before I'm lulled to sleep by the smooth rumble of the old truck.

CHAPTER 16

Shaw

She just left! I pace the floor in my bedroom, where I still smell sex, and her. After the amazing week we spent together, she just left, with hardly a good-bye. Maybe I had completely misread the situation, and it was just sex. I mean, we were trapped to-gether with little to do. It's a fun way to pass time, and we have amazing sexual chemistry. Maybe we both didn't want the same things? Maybe my age is a bigger deal to her than it is to me? Or maybe what her dad thinks is the end-all-be-all? He certainly didn't seem to like the age difference, or that I was her boss. I shake my head. I obviously thought way too much into this.

Now that there is a pathway cleared for my truck, I pack up the bags I brought with me and get ready to head back to the penthouse. The power kicked back on earlier this morning, so I make sure all the lights are off. I dress in a Henley and jeans with my boots, and throw on a hoody and a beanie. I make sure that everything is off in the kitchen, turn off the gas to the stove, and unplug the fridge after loading the meager items left into a cooler. We really were running low on food. I walk over to the wood stove and put that fire out completely, making sure it's fully out before I make sure everything else is set. I load my bags and the cooler into the truck and lock everything up thoroughly.

I make my way out and get into the warmed-up truck. I look at the cabin in my rearview. I won't be able to walk back in there without thinking of her, without picturing her under me on almost every surface in there, without hearing her soft sighs as she snuggles into me before falling asleep at night. I take a deep breath and drive down the long drive to the main drag. I realize I'm going to miss her. Miss having her in my space. Miss having her in my arms as I fall asleep. Not just for the sex, but for the company she brings. The companionship and fun. She brought a light into my life that had been absent for most of it. I just wandered through life doing my *duty*. She brought happiness to my otherwise complacent life.

An hour out of the city, I call Jessica. "Hello, Hutchens & Co, Jessica speaking," she says, her tone professional.

"Hey Jess, It's Shaw. I was calling to tell you to reinstate Aleice Taylor to the cyber department and I would like to give her a raise and a bonus for not only what we put her through, but for also finding the evidence on the person who actually committed the crime. She will replace Jace's position." I growl out the last part. Hating that he took from me, from my company, that he stalked and scared Aleice.

"Of course, sir. Is there a number you were thinking?" she replies after a few moments of hesitation.

Once we get everything worked out, I let her know Aleice will be in tomorrow and to have the papers ready to sign, and say goodbye.

I get home and pull into the underground parking lot. I grab my bags and the cooler and carry them over to the elevator, taking it up to the top floor. The door opens and I'm caught in the silence. It seems to echo in the house. I huff out a breath and step off the elevator. Maybe I should have just gone out tonight. Gotten a few drinks in me to fill the loneliness.

Glancing at the clock, I see it's already six. I wander into the kitchen and see the fridge is fully stocked. The housekeeper takes care of that for me. I'm going to miss Aleice's home cooking. Fuck, she was an excellent cook. I grab some dry noodles and make myself some pasta with sauce. Nothing near as good as anything she had made, but it'll do. I turn on the TV just to have some sound, to drown out the silence that is so loud its deafening—the emptiness all encompassing.

I head to the office after dinner to get caught up on some work. Being off for over a week, I've fallen way behind. But I know the company was in excellent hands with Reed. I kept him posted on what was going on and he had no problem filling in. It feels weird to hand it off like that. I've always done all the work myself. I struggle to delegate, I have a way I like things done.

After spending a few hours making sure all the Ts are crossed and the Is are dotted to my specifications, I head back to the living room and make my way to the liquor cabinet to fix myself a drink. After shooting the first two glasses of Jameson back like shots, I enjoy the flavor of the last one.

I head to my room, stripping off my clothes as I go, leaving a trail behind me before falling back into the bed. Reaching into the nightstand, I pull out the thin lace panties that still smell like Aleice. She left them behind during our first night together. I'm not sure why I didn't give them back to her, especially when I hated her... but now I'm glad I didn't. I bring the small fabric to my nose before breathing in her sweet smell. "Shit," I say as I reach down and stroke my now hardening cock. I want to wrap it around my cock and jerk myself into it, but then I will have to wash her scent off it. Instead, I picture her at the cabin, walking around in my shirt, her nipples hard and poking through the fabric. I hear the mewls she made when I sucked them into my mouth. I can still taste her when I worked my tongue through her soft pink folds, and I remember how wet she would get for me. I squeeze my cock in my fist to mimic how tight she felt around me before using the pre-cum I had milked out to lube up my cock. Working my fist from root to tip, I picture how good it felt to be inside her, her sexy body as she thrashed under me whenever I sunk to the hilt. How she rubbed her hands all over my body, almost reverently, how her eyes would glaze over at the sight of my cock pumping in and out of her tight cunt. Her moans echo in my ears as I feel my release building before it explodes out of me. Rope after rope covers my hand and stomach. After I catch my breath, I walk over to the bathroom and clean myself off before climbing back into bed and letting sleep take me. Hopefully she won't visit me in my dreams.

* * *

The next day I head into the HR office, hoping to run into Aleice. I walk into Jessica's office to see if I've missed her.

"Hey Jess, have you seen Miss Taylor yet?" I ask, trying to keep my voice level like I'm just here to take care of business.

Her eyes narrow as she looks at me, then she plasters on a smile and says, "Nope. To be honest, I'm not sure she even showed up for work yet today." She shrugs like it makes no difference to her.

I furrow my own brows but figure it's still early. Maybe she just hasn't made it up here yet. "All right well, let me know if you see her."

Her lip lifts slightly in a sneer before she quickly covers it up. "Of course."

I ignore her strange reaction and make my way back to my office. I sit back down in my chair and turn my computer on before bringing up our clock-in program for today. Sure enough, she isn't in yet. "Huh," I grunt. Maybe she decided it was too uncomfortable with me being her boss after the week we spent together to come back. After all, she has that app. She can finish it and sell, and be set for life. She doesn't need me or this company, it seems. I quickly shut the program and get to work, deciding it's better to not focus on her anymore. Not needing any more of a distraction.

The day drags on and I may have checked the check-in area three more times throughout the day. Still nothing. With my suspicions confirmed, I decide I'm done with her. If I was so forgettable, then I can make her forgettable too… somehow.

CHAPTER 17

Aleice

I open my eyes in complete darkness. My head is pounding, and my face feels wet and cold. What the fuck is going on?

The last thing I remember is dad dropping me off and walking into my apartment. Jamie was gone at work, and I went straight for the shower, wanting to wash away the remanence of the dream that is Shaw.

I lift myself off the cold ground and try to make sense of anything around me. My eyes are having a hard time adjusting, so I reach out carefully with my arms to feel for anything around me. Nothing. Where am I? I reach up and wipe my face to find it is, in fact, wet. My glasses are gone. Feeling around on the ground, I find a puddle where I had been lying. My clothes are soaked. I continue to feel around, hoping my glasses just feel off somewhere, but I can't find them. "Fuck," I murmur, barely a whisper.

After an undetermined amount of time, I hear what sounds like the rattles of a key in a lock. A door opens and the bright light momentarily blinds me. I yelp and cover my eyes from the burn.

"Wakey, wakey, sleeping beauty," a rough voice calls from the direction of the door. It sounds familiar and yet different, rawer and raspier than before, like gravel is stuck in his throat.

Chancing a glance, I blink rapidly to get my eyes to adjust. When they finally do, the blur of Jace stands in the open doorway with a tray of something in his hands. He takes a few steps toward me, and I scurry back to keep the distance between us. He's close enough now for me to see him clearly without my glasses.

"J.. J.. Jace, what are you doing? W.. why am I here?" I stutter out in a panic, fear rising so rapidly in my stomach I think I might puke.

"Oh, don't be coy with me, baby. You know exactly why you're here." He licks his lips and kneels down in front of me to place the tray down. Not looking at it, I stare directly at him. His eyes are dark and reflect only madness. He whispers, "You're mine, have been for years, and although my plan had been pushed forward thanks to that old pain in my ass," he sneers out, "I made some... modifications and here you are." He finishes, waving his arm like ta-da.

He looks down at the tray that I still haven't even glanced at and frowns, "Eat my angel, you will need your strength." His smile is twisted and unhinged. Fuck, fuck, fuck. I am in a shit ton of trouble right now. I panic as my brain spins around, trying to figure out how to get out of here.

"I have to pee," I announce, hoping that might be my escape. His smile remains as he points to a bucket in the corner. I shake my head. "No!" I look directly at him, and his smile widens before his manic laugh cuts through the air.

"Oh, I know about your aversion to public bathrooms," he chuckles as he runs his hand over my jaw before running it through my hair. I try to jerk back, but he grabs my hair yanking me to him. "This is my punishment to you for ruining my carefully orchestrated plan. You were supposed to be with me. *Not Shaw!*" he growls in my face. "Now eat up," he says, his voice back to the way he used to speak to me at the office, as if he didn't just have a mental breakdown seconds before. He stands and turns to leave. Right before he makes it to the door, he says, "Oh, and don't try anything stupid. I'm watching you." He smiles as he points to the camera mounted in the corner by the door. He leaves, closing the door behind him, and locks it.

My heart rate is through the roof and I'm pretty sure I'm having a heart attack. I breathe in deep and hold it for a few seconds before letting it out. I continue this over and over until I feel myself relax slightly and my heart rate return to normal. I need to think logically. I need to use my brain. With an IQ of 163, I should be able to think my way out of this situation. I rock back and forth as I consider my options, any option, trying to keep my thoughts from spiraling out of control and the panic from taking over.

Okay, so he likes me and wants me. I should be able to use that to my advantage, right? Hopefully, he likes me enough that he won't physically hurt me. I cringe.

There is a soft bulb that keeps flickering in the room. Just bright enough to see vague shapes around me. Glancing down at the food, my stomach grumbles. I have no clue if it's poisoned or not. I rub my hands back and forth over my face. Fuck, what am I going to do? I want to be strong enough to fight him off if the need arises, but I also don't want to risk being drugged and have him do whatever he wants with me while I'm unconscious.

I tuck my knees to my chest and continue to rock back and forth, needing the comfort. I glance at the water bottle. I grab it and try the cap, feeling the whole thing for any hole where he might have injected something into it. There is nothing, and the top clicks as I break the seal. I take small sips. I know I need water to survive, but I also really don't want to pee in a bucket. I cringe at the thought of it. I know I'll do it if I need to, but the thought of him watching me pee in the bucket makes my skin crawl. Fucking dude is a psycho.

I try to look for any window or sign of light to show what time of day it is. How long was I out cold? A few hours? Days? Oh God, what if he already did stuff to me while I was out the first time? No! I shake my head and don't let that thought settle. *Don't let your brain go there*, I reprimand myself.

"If I'm yours, then why are you keeping me in here?" I say before my brain-to-mouth filter fully kicks in. I probably shouldn't say anything. It might be better in here than out there with him. But the need for answers is overwhelming, and still I get no response.

Eventually, I lean up against the wall and, after fighting it off for as long as possible, I finally succumb to sleep.

* * *

I don't know exactly how long I've been here, but it must have been days by now. He has come and gone four times, only bringing one tray each time. I only drink the water if it's sealed, and I did finally eat one granola bar when my stomach was cramping so hard I couldn't take the pain anymore. I had to use the bucket and died a little inside as I did. As the days go by, I lose more and more hope of getting out of here.

The only thing keeping me going is the thought that Shaw might notice I'm gone. He has a team of men at his disposal who handle situations like this. Even if he doesn't want me, surely, he would be at least a little worried when I didn't show up for work, right? And what about my dad? I can't leave him all alone; it would devastate him. I try to devise a plan. He comes in only once and he closes the door behind him. I've tried to engage him in conversation, to get answers out of him, but he seems determined to make me pay for whatever wrongs he thinks I've committed. I've looked around the room, but it's completely empty of anything I could use as a weapon or in self-defense. If I'm going to attack him, I need to get it right the first time because I won't get a second try.

CHAPTER 18

Aleice

The days are blurring together. I am having a hard time keeping track. I understand now why people in captivity mark dashes on the walls.

I hear his heavy footfalls as he stomps down the stairs before he gets to the door. I hold my breath, never knowing what to expect when he enters.

"Aleice, my beautiful pet. I've come baring gifts, my love." He walks toward me until I'm forced to tilt my head all the way back to look up at him from my spot on the floor. I leave my expression blank, not giving him an inch.

"Oh, come on my little doll, you like gifts, don't you?" His voice drips with depravity. He shakes a box in front of me. I glance around the room, anything to not look directly at him.

"Why did you stalk me?" I whisper. I need clarity. Why is this happening?

"Aww, baby. I did it because from the second I saw you, I knew you were mine." He says it pragmatically, like it's the most obvious answer.

I shake my head slightly, as I think about all those times I felt followed, watched. All the time I spent looking over my shoulder. It was all him and his weird sense of entitlement to me.

"Why now? Why did you wait so long to take me, then?" Part of this, I realize, is morbid fascination. I can feed his ego and maybe his obsession with me if it gets me out of here.

"Hmm. I wanted to make sure we wouldn't be found, and we could live our lives together in peace. But in order to do that, I needed money; I had been slowly taking the money from those idiots for years without them noticing. I even had this cabin," he gestures around us with his arms, "set up to look like your father's cabin. I thought you would enjoy that." He smiles big enough to show his teeth.

Oh, God. There is not a brain cell in that head of his that is firing on all cylinders.

"I have been watching you, doll. I've been protecting you. Hell, I even got you the job at Hutchens & Co." He spits. "I've done everything for *you*, my love."

"What do you mean, you got me the job at Hutchens?" I stare at him with shock.

A smirk lights his face. "You think you just found them by coincidence?" he chortles. My heart sinks at the thought of how deep this is running. "I made sure you saw the ads on a ton of the primary sites you visit. Made sure to drop subtle hints to make you apply for the job. I knew Reed would be in. You're not only great with computers, but you're also pretty." His lip raises at the idea of another man finding me pretty. "Turns out once Jess found out you had been with Shaw, after years of trying to get him to notice her," he throws his head back and chuckles, "she wanted you gone so bad she even sucked my cock to make it happen. Sorry about that, by the way, but since I couldn't have you yet, I needed something." He rambles on, talking animatedly with his hands. "So we set the little 'Frame Aleice' plan in motion."

"But none of that matters now, my pet... We are together and I will finally have you." His eyes are manic as they trace my body, as if he can't wait to get his hands on me. I force myself to stand.

"You are MINE..." he growls out, the energy shifting around him as his excitement builds.

Fuck... fuck... how am I going to get out of this? He reaches for me, and I dart to the left, trying to dodge his hands, but it's no use. He's too close. His arm wraps around my waist and he drags me flush against him.

"Don't run, little doll. I'll always chase you... and I'll always find you," he whispers, his lips rubbing over my ear as his hot breath slides across my face.

His free hand slides into my hair, gripping it firmly in his hand before he bites his way down my jaw. I shiver in disgust at his touch, at his arm tightly around my waist, as it slides up until he's palming my breast. I swallow repeatedly to keep my bile from escaping my mouth.

He groans. "Yesssss... my pet. You're just as soft as I imagined. All those times standing outside of your window. Watching you undress." He groans again as he works his stiffness against my backside. I try to turn my face away from him, but with his hands pulling my hair, I don't have any give to move. He continues to work himself roughly against me until he moans and shutters a few times, finding his release. My shoulders lurch as I gag. With nothing in my stomach, all that comes up is the little water I drank earlier.

"Now look what you made me do, little pet." His smile is mischievous as he points at the huge jizz stain on the front of his pants. I quickly glance away so he doesn't see the disgust on my face. "I can't wait to take you properly." His face sours. "You just had to fuck that dusty old fart, didn't you? You had to ruin it, DIDN'T YOU!" He screams as he leans into my face. I flinch back in fear, at his mood flipping back and forth so drastically.

His hand flies out as he quickly wraps it around my throat. "Tell me Aleice, did you like it? Did you like him?" he sneers, spit flying out of his mouth and landing on my face. I turn my head from his assault and he tightens his hand around my throat, forcing the air from my lungs. "I won't ask again, little doll," he forces out through clenched teeth.

"No," I force the lie past my lips with the precious little air I have left. His whole body relaxes, and he loosens his hold. I gasp for air, drawing as much as I can into my deprived lungs.

"Of course not. You've always loved me." He murmurs to himself.

He backs away from me and paces back and forth, mumbling nonsense to himself. I take a few deep breaths without him in my face. I try to creep along the wall towards the door. He stops and his eyes connect with mine before he tilts his head to the side, studying me. I hold my breath, waiting to see what he does.

"What are you doing, little doll?" he asks, his voice void of any emotion at all. I swallow audibly before glancing around. My eyes land on the bucket that happens to be in the right direction. Noticing where I looked, he nods his head. "Go ahead, little doll, don't mind me." He cackles as he widens his stance and crosses his arms across his chest. Oh, God. No. I'm already shaking my head. There is no way I can pee in front of him. I can't even pee in a public bathroom. How am I supposed to do it with this creepy fuck standing there? The only reason I could go at work was because I was the only woman on that floor to use the women's restroom. "You weren't trying to run, were you doll?" He smirks, and I realize he's calling my bluff.

I slowly make my way over to the bucket before lowering the sleep shorts that he brought me here in, just enough so I don't pee on them, and I lower myself to the bucket. Clenching my eyes as tight as I can. I can feel his presence lingering and his eyes burning a hole in me. I can't fucking do it.

After a few moments, he laughs. "That's what I thought." He steps forward and rips me up off the bucket by my hair. I scream as the pain sears through my skull like someone just lit it on fire. Scrambling to try to pull my shorts up the short distance so he can't see me. I get myself covered before he throws me on the floor. "Get it through your head. You. Are. Not. Going. Anywhere." He punctuates each word while roaring at me.

"I'm sorry," I whisper once he's silent. The air pulses with his anger, almost tangible.

"I won't keep playing these games with you, Aleice." He growls as he takes a few steps back before turning and heading toward the door. When he gets there, he takes one last glance back at me on the floor before shaking his head and slamming the door behind him.

I take a deep breath, thankful that he's gone. I've never been happier to be alone in my life. How did I think this guy was attractive at one point? I shake my head. How did I not see that this guy has more than a few screws loose? I shiver at the thought of him watching me all those times, my privacy completely taken from me.

As I lean back against the cold concrete floor, I tuck my knees to my chest and, for the first time since I've been imprisoned, I cry. Big, wet tears roll down my cheeks as I contemplate how I got here. How the fuck did this happen? I need to get out of here. I choke on a sob as I think about Shaw. I never got to tell him how I feel, that I want to be with him. Now I may never get the chance. Another sob rips from my throat at that thought.

After I have literally cried myself dry of tears, I feel my eye lids droop and my body shut down with exhaustion. *I need to find a way out, a way back to him*, is my last thought before I finally pass out.

CHAPTER 19

Shaw

It's been a week since I've seen Aleice. She still hasn't shown up for work. I've tried driving by her apartment and noticed the lights on, so I'm assuming she's there and just wants nothing to do with me anymore. It doesn't seem like her, to make a big deal out of me firing her and her clearing her name just to give up when she finally got the job back. But what do I know? I also thought she wanted more than just sex. I shake my head.

It's early Saturday morning when my phone rings. I don't recognize the number, so I hit the ignore button and roll back over. Soon after, the phone rings again with the same number. I glance over at the clock on my nightstand and see it's five in the morning. Who the fuck calls someone at five in the morning?

"Hello?" I grumble into the phone, my voice rough with sleep.

"Have you seen Aleice?"

I sit up in bed, readjusting the phone on my ear. "Who is this?" I ask, suddenly wide awake.

"It's Jamie, Aleice's roommate. I'm sorry to be calling you so early, but I figured since she hasn't come home that she was with you."

My breath stalls in my chest. "What?" I ask, because clearly, I haven't heard her correctly.

"She hasn't been home. I see some dirty clothes in her laundry basket and a towel in her shower that wasn't there, but I haven't seen *her*, and she still doesn't have a phone."

My mind instantly goes to Jace, to the stalking. "Fuck!" I shout as I end the call and immediately call my team. Two of them were on jobs, but I've called the other six. "We need to find him, now!" I growl down the line to my team.

Reed answers when everyone else stays silent. "How? We have no clue of his whereabouts. The information on all of his work documents all go to a P.O box and we haven't been able to trace his IP address. He keeps pinging it off other locations."

Fuck, it's like looking for a needle in a haystack. He could have her out of the country by now. "I'll call you back." I hang up.

I pace around my room before making my way to my office and starting up the computer. Fuck. Think, think. Where would that sick fuck take her?

I try to break down what I know about Jace. He's good at computers. With all the money he stole, he could move around easily, and could leave the state quickly. Fuck, probably even the country. But would he? I rub my forehead in frustration before tugging at my hair with both hands. "FUCK!" I growl out, feeling hopeless.

After ten minutes of pacing, my cell phone rings with the auto repair shop's number coming up.

"Hello?" I answer, curious why they are calling me so early.

"Sorry to disturb you sir, but you had asked us to call you as soon as possible with updates on the Maxima. I just got into the shop and the boys who looked at it last night left me a note. There was a bullet hole in the back right tire. The car most likely didn't slide on the ice, but the tire blew, and the driver lost control. I mean, I wasn't at the scene of the accident, so I couldn't be certain, but that's my best guess based on where the damage to the car is."

My blood runs cold. The fucker shot at her car. Was he aiming for her? Is he that crazy that, if he couldn't have her, no one could? Was he going to grab her then, had I not intervened? All these thoughts go rushing through my head, but I don't have any answers.

"Was the bullet still there?" I ask, hopeful we might have caught a break.

"Yes, sir, we retrieved the bullet," he says, slightly confused. "We are going to turn it into the police, sir," he says, hesitating.

"Yes, but first I need to see it. I'll be there in ten minutes to get it," I say before hanging up without a goodbye.

I race down the hall and back to my room, grabbing a shirt and a pair of jeans. I rush and get dressed before tossing on my shoes and grabbing the keys to my truck. I anxiously wait as I call the elevator. "Fuck!" I roar as it seems to take forever when, in reality, it was probably only a few moments. Once the doors open, I launch myself inside and slam the button for the underground lot.

Pulling my phone from my pocket, I dial Reed's number. He answers on the first ring. "Hey, they found a bullet in her back tire. He thinks that was what caused the accident, not the ice. I'm heading there now to see if I can get a serial number off it. I'll meet you at your place. I'm going to need you to do a little hacking and whatever the fuck it is you do," I say before he even gets hello out.

"Okay, and Shaw…"

I pause for a minute to listen to what he has to say.

He seems to rethink it and goes with, "we will get her back safe, man," and the line disconnects.

Fuck, we better or I might just go to prison for murder.

The elevator doors open, and I race to my truck before hopping in and backing out. I hit the gas pedal as I peel out. I drive as fast as I can to the repair shop without killing anyone. I get there in eight minutes. I slam the truck into park and hop out before banging on the shop door. I know I need to chill the hell out or this guy is going to call the cops, but my mind is too focused on Aleice and whatever the sick fuck might be doing to her.

The older man opens the door, his eyes wide. "Good morning, Shaw." He hesitates a second before opening the door wider for me to step in.

"Mornin' Danny. I'm sorry for barging in here, but we think the guy who shot this bullet might have kidnapped the woman as well. My security team is trying to track her down now, but with no leads, we are dead in the water. The bastard has had her for six days now and we need to get to her as soon as possible." I stare him right in the eyes, pleading with him to understand.

He looks at me for a second longer before nodding. He hands over the bag with the bullet. "This is more than just another mission, ain't it, son?" he says, a knowing look in his eyes.

"Yes, sir. Once I get the serial number off the bullet and see if we can trace it back to an address, I'll call it in to the police, but hopefully by then she will be back home safe," I tell him.

"I'm still going to call it in on my end, don't want nothing coming back on me or the shop guys," he tells me with a stern look.

"That's fine. All I ask is you give me twenty-four hours," I plead.

He stares at me as if judging my character. "All right," he concedes before he makes a shewing motion with his hands. "Times a'wastin'."

Without anything more said, I turn and head back to my truck before hauling ass over to Reed's house.

I don't even knock before bursting in through the front door. A girl yelps as she clutches a shirt that must be Reed's to her chest. Reed comes sauntering out of his bedroom in just a pair of sweats. He smirks as he scratches his chest.

"Ever hear of knocking, asshole," he snarks before smacking the girl on the ass and whispering something in her ear that has her giggling before heading back to the bedroom.

"I told you I was coming, dipshit," I say. I don't have time for this. I walk over and show him the bullet. "We need to trace the serial number and see if we can get his actual address from the shop where he purchased the gun." I am all but pushing him toward his home office to his computer.

"Jesus dude, I know she's our employee and all, but can't the cops handle this?" he asks me as he takes a seat at his computer, moving at a glacial pace.

"NO!" I growl at him. His eyes widen as he takes me in.

After a moment, a smirk lights his face. "You're fucking her, aren't you?" He throws his head back and laughs, and I try very hard not to punch him in the throat.

"Can we laugh and joke about it later when she hasn't been kidnapped by a fucking psychopath." I hold my arms out, my face red with rage.

He quickly sobers and nods his head. "Right sorry…" He types away on his computer before grabbing the bullet. After typing around for about ten minutes, he looks up at me triumphantly. He points to the screen. We got him.

CHAPTER 20

Aleice

I don't know how long I've been here; I only know that it feels like forever. I have eaten the food, but I can't keep much of it down. The nausea is constant. I still haven't left this basement, but he's coming in more and more now and I miss the days when it was just once. He brings in clothes and dresses me up in different outfits, like his own personal doll. I tried to resist the first few times, but after seeing the dangerous glint in his eyes and the way his palms twitched, I just started putting the clothes on. At least all he does is take pictures of me in them. I cringe, but it could be worse.

The door opens and the light from the opening casts over me as I sit on the cold, hard floor.

"Up, up my beauty," he purrs as he carries over another outfit. So far, he hasn't tried anything sexual other than that one incident, and I haven't been in less than my bra and panties.

"I need to shower, please Jace," I beg as my stomach tightens and I pitch over in pain. He waits for a second, debating this. I don't want to shower in front of him, but I've come to terms with the fact that I'm most likely not getting out of here. The one time I tried to escape, I made it as far as the door at the top of the stairs before he yanked me back and didn't feed me for two days as punishment. Seeing him now look my body up and down as a slow smile grows on his evil face makes me think twice about trying anything again.

"Okay, my pet, you can shower." Before I can process what he just said, he grabs my wrist and lifts me off the floor before tossing me over his shoulder. I kick and flail my arms, trying to do as much damage to his organs as possible, but he just chuckles. "I like that you haven't lost your fight. I will break you soon enough and then you will be *all* mine," he whispers reverently into my hip before biting me there. I try to squirm away, but up high on his shoulder, there is nowhere to go. He carries me up the stairs and unlocks that door before carrying me through a living room that looks very similar to my father's cabin. The furnishings are different, and the layout is the opposite, but other than that, it's the same. He walks to the bathroom down the hallway from the bedrooms and dumps me on the floor.

I fall back onto my ass, my tailbone smacking the tile floor hard. I hiss as the pain radiates through my back. He closes the door and stands in front of it. Suddenly, the idea of getting clean isn't as appealing. He looks down at me on the floor and I see the bulge in his pants growing.

"I like you beneath me." He raises an eyebrow and takes a step toward me. I use my arms to scramble back away from him in the small space. "Go ahead, little doll, take a shower," he taunts, and I suddenly wish I never brought it up. It's just with shitting in a bucket and puking for days, the thought of the brief reprieve of a shower sounded like a bit of heaven in this hell. I should have known the fucker wouldn't give me any space. My stomach turns and I yank the toilet seat up before emptying the contents of my stomach into the bowl. His brows furrow as he takes me in. I look at my arms and realize I've lost weight since I've been here. My arms are much smaller with what little food I've eaten, and all the vomiting. He must have some pity on me because he turns the shower on, then turns around and heads for the door.

"I'll be right outside listening, pet, so don't

do anything stupid," he growls as he strokes my hair back. I cringe away from him, and he smiles. He leaves and I hear a thunk sound as he leans back against the door.

Once he's gone, I quickly undress and get into the shower. I sit on the ground and let the water run over me as tears run down my face. I miss Shaw. I wonder if he's looking for me. Probably not, I'm just the girl he had a fun week with, an extended one-night stand. I bury my face in my hands as the sobs rock my body. I have to stay strong. I have to fight; I can't give up and let him have me. I have my dad to think about—he needs me. With that thought in mind, I stand up on shaky legs and wash my hair and body, the water slightly relieving the nausea. I squeeze my eyes shut and focus on formulating a plan. Now that I'm upstairs, all I need to do is get past him, and I could run for the front door. But without warm clothes, and not knowing where the fuck I am, how am I supposed to get far enough away from him? I'm so tired, unable to get adequate rest with the knowledge of him looming over me, watching my every move. My body is drained, weak from lack of food and sleep. I try to hold it together, to not feel hopeless. I *won't* let him break me.

Turning off the water, I grab the towel that's hanging on the hook and dry myself off. It's then I notice he must have put some clothes by the sink. Normal clothes this time, jeans and a t-shirt, along with clean panties and a bra. I try not to think about how he knew my size and instead get dressed quickly, thankful to be in something clean.

Enjoying a few more moments of peace, I take deep breaths before he opens the door and I'm faced with him again. He looks me up and down and smiles.

"This has always been my favorite look," he murmurs, almost to himself. He grabs my wrist and pulls me out to the living room. He forces me down to the floor between the couch and the coffee table before he sits behind me on the couch and squeezes his legs around my body.

I shake, unsure of what he's going to do to me. Fear has my stomach clenching tight and my heart racing. A moment later, he pulls my hair back away from my face. I squirm to try to free my arms but it's no use, his legs are stronger. He slowly starts working a brush through my hair, careful not to snag any tangles. I freeze, unsure of what the fuck is going on.

He takes his time working the brush through all the knots until my hair is smooth, then he braids it before tying it off with a hair tie. I sit stock still and silent, not sure what to do with this sudden gentleness. It has to be a trick or something.

Once he's finished, he stands and walks over

to the kitchen that's all open so he can watch me from where he stands. I glance around the space some more, cataloging everything I can to memory, trying to find something I can use as a weapon, all while considering how many steps it would be for me to get to the door versus him getting there before me. All I see that I can use are the lamps on the end tables.

I look over at him to watch what he's doing, and I see him staring directly at me. He's testing me. He wants to see what I'll do with a little freedom. I slowly stand and I see him stand up taller and his body tightens. I take careful steps toward the kitchen. Maybe I can sneak a knife. I make sure to not make any sudden movements as I walk beside him. I take a deep breath. Time to implement my plan. I slide my hand along his back, trying to hold back my gag reflex. I take another deep breath —just a little further. I slide my other hand up and down his back. I feel him relax into my touch and I hear a small groan of appreciation leave his lips. I wrap my arms around his waist as if I'm giving him a hug from behind. I feel his abs tighten as he sucks in a breath.

"I knew you'd come around. I knew you felt it, too," he whispers and his hands clench against the countertop and his eyes slide closed. I peer around him and see he's filled two bowls full of some kind of stew. It actually smells delicious and I'm kind of sad I won't be able to eat it. I work my hand lower, feeling his stiffness straining against his fly.

"Oh, God... yes... my little doll," he moans as I continue to stroke him outside of his pants.

I bite my tongue to hold in the bile. My other hand slides onto the counter until I can wrap my fingers around the chopping knife he used for the vegetables. I moan loudly to cover the sound of my grabbing it off the counter. At the sound of my moan, I feel his cock twitch in his jeans, and he doubles over as he ejaculates. Using the distraction, I pull the knife back and with both hands, I thrust it into his back.

"AHHHH!" he yells as the blade enters his back almost to the hilt. He whips around, but I'm already a few steps toward the front door.

Maybe I should have gone for something a little more debilitating. Fuck. I don't even have shoes on, but fuck it. I get to the door and try to turn the knob but it's locked.

"FUCK!" I scream in frustration as he runs at me. I turn so my back is to the door and kick out with my foot. I have not come this far just to get stuck. I catch him right in the gut with my foot, giving me a little room to move to the left and into the living room. I grab the lamp off the table. He turns toward me and chuckles, but he's panting now with excursion.

"What are you going to do with that?" He reaches for it, but I move to the side, and he narrowly misses. I readjust my hands and swing back at him and it smashes across his head. I see him wobble a bit before he drops to his knees, his eyes shutter closed as he falls completely to the floor. He's out.

Wasting no time, I dig through his pockets for the key. Once I have it, I race to the door and unlock it, throwing it open. The first thing I see is snow. "Fuck... this is going to suck," I say, just as I take off running barefoot into the snow. My feet instantly register the cold before the burning starts. I whip my head around to try to get my bearings.

Holy fuck! I know where I am... I head northwest, running as fast as I can. Not only will he be able to see my footsteps if he follows, but he will most likely know where I'm heading.

My lungs burn with the cold air that's racing in and out as I run as fast as I can. The snow is up to the middle of my calf, so I'm having to pick my knees up as I go. I can't feel my face and my feet burn like they are on fire. I shiver and shake as I reach the front steps before lifting the mat and finding the spare key, opening the door to dad's cabin. I close and lock it behind me. I race to the landline, thanking my lucky stars my dad is old school. The first person I think to call is Shaw. Even if he hates me, he will still help, right? Dialing his number, it rings through with no response. "Fuck, Fuck, Fuck! Why is it whenever you need someone they don't answer!" I screech in panic as I hear banging up the steps. God, he's here.

I hit redial and send up a prayer that someone is with me.

"Hello." I hear a growl down the line.

"Shaw... Shaw... help me," I pant, panic so thick in my voice I'm almost choking on it. "Aleice, where are you?" "I'm at Dad's cabin, just off North Creek, about five miles south of yours." I say the address so fast, I'm not sure he could even understand. The door shakes on its hinges as his boot connects to it.

"Shaw, he's going to kill me. Please help me," I beg

"I'm on my way baby, hold on!" he growls.

The door flies open then, and Jace's snow-covered boots crunch across the floor. I drop the phone and run. I can't go outside again; I'm already risking hyperthermia. I force my feet to move, despite not being able to feel them. I make my way to the back bedroom, close the door and lock it behind me. It won't stop him, but it will buy me some time. I run to dad's closet and bend down to enter the code to the safe. Thank God he hasn't changed it and it's still my birthday. The safe beeps with the correct code and I open the door to pull out the handgun and ammo. I quickly load the gun, sending up another prayer of thanks that my southern father taught me how to shoot a gun. The door slams against the wall as he swiftly kicks it in.

"YOU BITCH!" Jace yells before taking a step in the room, before I hear *pop... pop... pop.*

CHAPTER 21

Shaw

She's dropped the phone. That much I can tell because everything else is muffled until I hear the telltale sound of a gun going off. Pop... pop... pop. My heart hammers in my chest, fearing the worst. I'm not going to make it in time. I scream her name down the line.

At the address just outside of the city, Reed and I were able to get inside, after a little breaking and entering. Walking in was like walking into a shrine of Aleice. Pictures of her line the walls like wallpaper in every room. Pictures of her in all sorts of states of dress. To see her beautiful body on display for this creeper made my blood boil. He invaded her privacy. He had pairs of her panties and old Starbucks cups with her name on them. He has followed her for years, no doubt in my mind. He had a schedule on the wall of her day-to-day activities. We were already headed up to another address up on Kilburn, to which we found some mail addressed, when she called.

I slam the pedal to the floor as I race through traffic on the highway. I'm breaking so many traffic laws right now, but I can't find it in me to give a shit. Reed is in the passenger's seat on his laptop. I'm pretty sure he's checking the police scanners.

"We're clear," he says as he closes his laptop.

I take the exit for the mountain on my right and run the red light there before turning right and heading up the mountain. We are still about fifteen minutes away.

"She could be bleeding out!" I roar as I round the corner and run through at least three more lights.

"I've already notified the police, and they are five minutes out," Reed states matter-of-factly.

I continue to pick up speed on all the straight aways, barely slowing down to take the turns.

"Chill the fuck out, Shaw, we can't help her if we never fucking make it there," he gripes as he clings to the oh-shit handle and the dashboard simultaneously. I ignore him and continue to haul ass. Thankfully, the roads are now clear. We get there just before the police pull up. I fling the door open and race into the house quickly, whipping my head around in search of her.

"Shaw... the police are going to arrest your dumbass," Reed yells from just outside the door.

I won't touch any evidence. I just need to make sure she's okay.

"Sir, we need you to exit the premises immediately."

"My girls in here!" I yell back to let them know I'm not coming out until I find her.

"I understand, sir, but this is an active crime scene. We need you to get out now."

Yeah, that's not fucking happening. I ignore their request and head down the hallway, where I see the door has been kicked off its hinges. I pick up speed.

I enter the room and see Jace's body face down on the ground in a pool of blood, a knife sticking out of his back. I quickly scan the room until I find what I'm looking for. Aleice is curled up in the closet, her knees to her chest as she slowly rocks back and forth. She holds a gun in her hands, still pointing in his direction. She is mumbling to herself, "I killed him," over and over.

Thank fuck, she's alive. I pant as I quickly scan her body looking for injuries and find none. Fuck, she's so strong. My baby fought her way out, and she won. I'm so fucking proud of her. She must be in shock because she doesn't see me until I am kneeling down directly in front of her.

"Shh… baby, I got you," I say as soothing as possible. Her eyes lift to mine, and I see her take in my face. I reach out and drag her into my arms, where she breaks down into tears.

The police enter the room behind me. "Sir, we are going to need you to step away from the woman now and put your hands behind your back."

Fuck me, why did we call the police again? Fucking useless. I do as they say and stand.

"No… no…" she whimpers as she reaches for me. "Please." Her lip trembles as she looks pleadingly at the police. "I need him, please." Tears spill over her lids and run down her face. "I'll tell you everything. Just please let him stay with me."

The police concede to her request, and they pull us both outside. Noticing she isn't wearing shoes or a jacket, I lift her into my arms and carry her over to where an ambulance now sits. They wrap her in a mylar blanket, and she sits in the back as they check her vitals.

The EMTs ask her a series of questions before determining she is in shock and she's at risk for hypothermia. They wrap her feet with chemical heating packs wrapped in cloth. The cops who arrived at the scene say they will follow us to the hospital and question her there while the rest of their team goes through the cabin.

We make it to the nearest hospital in record time, but since I'm not family or her husband, they don't allow me back with her, so I pace the waiting room instead. I should have just said I was her husband. Reed followed behind the ambulance and was now sitting in the chair drinking shitty hospital coffee.

"Calm the fuck down, Shaw." He rolls his eyes, clearly still not getting it. "It's not like she can sue us or anything. After all, we fired her before it happened." He chuckles.

I stop and stare directly at him with a look that I'm sure is close to what the reaper wears before he takes your soul to the underworld. I've never wanted to hurt someone more than at this moment.

He sees the look on my face and his smile drops and fear crosses his eyes.

"Let me make something really fucking clear. She isn't just some girl; she is *my* girl. And I'm not worried about her fucking suing us, you ass fuck. I'm worried about the fact that she could have been..." I can't even fucking say it. My gut turns, and the bile rises in my throat before I swallow it back down.

The shock registers on his face as he takes in what I said. "Wow man, I'm sorry. I didn't know." He raises his hands in surrender. I turn away from him and start pacing again so I don't do something stupid, like strangle him in a hospital.

Two hours later, the doctor comes out and makes his way over to me and Reed. "Hello, Mr. Hutchens?" he asks, looking down at the chart in his hands flipping through a few pages before looking at me again.

"Yes," I swallow hard, barely managing to get the word past my lips.

He must see the panic in my face because he quickly says, "She's fine. We got her limbs warmed up in time and, although she had frostnip in her feet, we were able to get them fully functioning again."

I take a huge sigh of relief before falling back into the chair. Holy fuck, she's okay. She's okay. She's okay.

"I'm sorry I can't tell you more, but the officers are in there with her now. Once they are done, you should be able to go in and talk to her yourself." The doctor glances one last time at the chart to make sure he hasn't forgotten anything. "If you have any questions ask one of the nurses and she can page me." He shakes my hand.

"Thank you so much," I say before he nods and turns, walking away. I rest my head back on the chair as I process that she's okay. I need to see her, to hold her, to let it sink in that she's all right.

After another hour, I see the police leave her room. I reach into my back pocket and as they go to pass me, I hand them the bag with the bullet from Jace's gun. "You're going to need this." The two cops look at each other before looking back at me. "It's the bullet the fucker used to shoot her tire out the week before he kidnapped her," I answer their unasked question.

The cop closest to me, Officer Bowen, nods his head to me before grabbing the bag and leaving. "Keep close, Mr. Hutchens," they say as they walk out through the hospital exit.

I race down the hall to room 203, her room. I quietly knock on the door before stepping inside and rounding the corner to the open room. I see her lying there, an IV in her arm and the beeping of the heart monitor, my heart clenching in response.

I should have gone to her apartment. I should have done more to protect her. Guilt rises in my gut as I stare at her thin body. How can someone lose so much weight in a week? I walk closer to her and reach for her hand.

At the contact, her eyes spring open. "Shaw," she whispers, a small smile gracing her face.

"I'm so glad you're safe, baby girl," I say, kissing the back of her hand before squeezing it tightly in mine.

"Me too." She smirks as she rubs her thumb across the back of my hand.

"W... w..." I clear my throat; I have to know. "What happened, baby?" I sit down on the edge of the bed and so I can hold both of her hands at once. "If it's too much, you don't have to tell me." I sense she's struggling, despite how fucking strong I think she is. Her eyes slightly glaze over. "I'm so fucking proud of you. You're so fucking strong, Ally, baby." I move closer to her and bring her in for a hug.

She rests her head on my shoulder, taking slow breaths at my neck. "You smell so good," she says as she burrows further into my chest.

I chuckle and rub my hands up and down her back. I kiss the top of her head as I feel her soft tears soaking through my shirt.

"He didn't hurt my physically. He just did some really creepy shit. And he didn't feed me much. They should really offer that as a new diet plan. Who needs weight watchers when you have creepy man watchers." She chuckles to herself, shaking her head.

I smirk as I watch her. She's utterly amazing. "You're mine," I say, because it's the only thing I can think of right now. How proud I am of my girl. Her head raises and her eyebrows hit her hairline.

"I thought... I thought it was just a one-time thing. I thought you didn't do serious relationships?" she asks as her eyes trace my face, hoping for answers. So much hope in her eyes as she waits for my answer.

"It could never just be a one-time thing with you, baby. You're everything to me. I can't picture spending my life without you by my side. My better half. Ally baby, I love you," I say as I grab her neck and stroke my thumb over her jaw.

Tears fall down her face again as she stares at me, mouth agape. "I love you too." She finally finds her words and crawls into my lap.

I hold her close and breathe her in. She's safe, she's okay, she's here. I kiss her, whispering, "I love you so much," against her lips before tapping my lips against hers three more times.

CHAPTER 22

Aleice

He loves me. It's all I can think as I snuggle into his warm lap, sucking up his affection. After a few moments, I hear another knock at the door. Reed and my dad walk in. I slide off Shaw's lap and back onto the bed. Before pulling the covers back up.

Reed stands at the back of the room, but dad takes a step toward me before grabbing my hand.

"Oh, bug." He looks at me like I'm going to break in half if he touches me.

"I'm sorry about the cabin," I say as I slide my eyes back over to Shaw.

Dad's brows furrow as he says, "Fuck the cabin."

I gasp in shock. My father hardly ever swears.

"But I'm glad it was there to keep you safe."

My eyes blur and I know the tears will soon spill. "It was like mom was looking out for me," I whisper so only he and Shaw can hear.

Dad smiles and pats my hand. "I have no doubt, bug, no doubt." He leans forward and kisses my head before he glances around. His eyes look back at my thin arms. "I'm going to find the closest fast food joint. We need to put some meat back on those bones." He smiles before making his way back out into the hallway. Dad has never been good in hospitals, ever since mom died.

Reed looks at me and says, "I'm glad you're okay," before making his exit as well.

It's just Shaw and me again when the nurse comes in to check my vitals and blood pressure. She looks down at the chart and nods her head. "Okay sweetheart, we got your blood work back." She looks up and sees Shaw sitting there and closes her mouth. "I'm sorry, sir, but would you mind stepping out for a moment? I can't discuss the patient's medical information with you presently." She smiles kindly at him.

"He can stay, he's my…" I pause. Should I call him boyfriend? Is that what we are? Friends?

"Fiancé," Shaw clarifies.

My jaw drops open at his proclamation. The nurse offers a knowing smile and looks at me again for clarification. I nod my head for her to proceed, not able to push any words through the lump in my throat.

"Honey, your bloodwork shows that you're pregnant. So, we would like to do an ultrasound to confirm baby's healthy." She heads back into the hallway, just to return a second later with an ultrasound machine.

I just sit there, no emotion on my face and I'm pretty sure I haven't blinked when she pulls the machine to the right side of the bed.

"Okay hun, I'm going to need you to lie back for me and lift your gown so I can get to your belly," she says as she grabs the clear gel off the cart and shakes it.

I do as she asks as if on autopilot. I finally am able to bring my eyes to Shaw's and he is staring at me, trying to gauge my reaction to the news. Slowly, a smile spreads onto my face before I tilt my head back and she squirts the gel onto my stomach before working the transducer over it. She moves it around for a bit before she pulls it away, wiping away the goop off with a towel. Oh, no, something's happened to the baby.

"You're just fine. I'm just going to need to have a tech come in and do a vaginal ultrasound. Since you're early in the pregnancy, sometimes it's hard to see this way. Okay?" she pats my hand and says, "Okay, I'm going to get a tech. I'll be back shortly." Then she leaves the room.

I take deep breaths, trying to remain calm. "You're going to be a daddy, and not just to me." I smile and wink. He laughs and the smile that lights up his face is unlike anything I've ever seen on him before.

"Going to be a daddy and a husband." He takes my hand and kisses where the engagement ring will be. "May have jumped the gun a little on that one," he says, looking at my bare finger. I giggle. "We can go pick one out together," he exclaims, smiling, kissing my mouth with so much passion I'm surprised we don't go up in flames. "Thank you," he says, placing kisses all over my face.

My brows furrow. "For what?" I ask, confused.

"For not only saving your life, but the one growing inside of you. I don't know what I would have done without you, baby. I'm so sorry it took my so long to find you." His eyes carry so much love and guilt.

"Baby, you couldn't have known where I was. I know if you had any clue, you would have found me." I reach for the back of his head and pull him to me. Wrapping my arms around him, I kiss his strong jaw, which no longer has a beard, but instead a five o'clock shadow. I reach up and rub his scruff. "I kind of miss the beard." I wiggle my eyebrows at him, and he chuckles.

"Whatever my girl wants, my girl gets." He kisses my forehead, and the ultrasound tech walks in.

"Hello," she says, waving slightly while walking over to the machine. She slips what looks like a condom onto the wand-like transducer and says, "Okay, I'm going to need you to raise your knees up for me."

I do as she asks, and she thankfully puts her arm under the covers to provide some modesty.

"Okay, I'm going to insert the wand now. You might feel a little pressure," she says right before she puts it in.

I chuckle to myself at the thought of 'pressure'. Considering the size of Shaw, I'd be surprised if I even feel it. Shaw glances at me and smirks, as if knowing what I am thinking. I wink and he nods. The tech is solely focused on the screen.

"There they are," she says as she points to

two blobs on the screen that resemble gummy bears. "You're about seven weeks along. Everything looks wonderful. Babies look healthy." She grabs a spinning wheel that shows months and days. "Looks like your due date is... August 27th. Congratulations mama!" She smiles at me while she quickly collects the machine and pulls it out of the room.

My brows furrow as I do the math on that. "Wait, if I'm seven weeks, then that means..." my eyes widen as I put two-and-two together. "We got pregnant that first night!" I turn to Shaw, my mouth open. "You wore a condom, though." I shake my head.

Shaw is silent and still and when I look back at him I see his eyes are on the little picture that the tech must have printed of the baby. I pick it up and climb back up onto his lap so we can look at it together. As my eyes focus in on the picture, I notice something strange.

"Ugh... Shaw?" I turn slightly and tilt my head back to look at his face, and I see a tear run down his cheek.

"There are two. Twins." The awe in his voice is evident.

"Yeah baby, there are. You ready for this, daddy?" I smile as I kiss my way up his neck before wrapping my arms around him.

He squeezes me back, and I can feel how happy he is through the hug. "I'm more than ready, baby. I can't wait to spend the rest of my life taking care of you and our babies." He tilts my chin and takes my lips in his, kissing me gentle before sliding his tongue along my bottom lip. I open for him, and he slides his tongue along mine slowly before twisting it and doing it again. He slides his hands into my hair and deepens the kiss.

"I'm so happy Ally, girl." He places me back in the bed and covers me up. I just stare at the picture and smile. Trying to wrap my head around the fact that, not only am I pregnant, but we are having twins.

EPILOGUE

Shaw

4 ½ years later

"Bub, have you seen the checkbook? Apparently, the bounce house people only take checks." She rolls her eyes. "Who doesn't take cards these days? I mean really." She huffs as she makes her way into the home office. I don't work hardly as much as I used to, but I still like to use the home office to pop in and make sure things are running smoothly.

"Yeah baby, they're right here." I tell her as I pull open the top drawer on my desk and hand it to her.

"Thanks daddy," she smiles and leans in to kiss me before taking off for the front door to pay the man. Just then, two little heads come flying into my office, jumping up and down.

"Dad, dad!" they yell together, because loud is the only volume they currently know. They are holding hands as they jump up and down. Our daughter Emma is wearing a cute little summer dress with her hair done up in braids and flower clips that she insists on pulling out of her hair every chance she gets. And Arlo, our son, is wearing a blue short-sleeve button up with little cargo shorts. They bounce up and down.

"What?!" I say back with excitement in my voice, like I don't already know what they are going to tell me.

"Mommy got us a bounce house for our burfday pawty," Arlo shouts as he turns and runs back out of the office. Emma stays behind—my shy one. She puts one hand out to me, showing she wants me to take it. Of course, I do. My kids have me wrapped around their little fingers. Almost as much as their mom does. She pulls me out into the kitchen, heading for the patio door to the backyard, where we find two guys blowing up a yellow, blue and red inflatable bounce house. The other kids will be showing up in about thirty minutes, and my amazing wife has taken care of every detail, making sure the twin's fourth birthday party is the best one yet.

I stand back and watch as my sexy, amazing wife takes charge. Her summer dress blows in the breeze, and the men setting up the house take notice. The flair of possession surges through me, but also a sense of pride at this extraordinary woman. She looks back and sees me standing in the doorway watching her, and her eyes slowly drag over my body before she reaches my face. Once she does, I see her bite her lip, then smile. She mouths *I love you*, before turning back to finish setting up the yard for the party.

I am constantly in awe of this woman. Four and a half years ago, after the whole Jace incident, I expected her to have some PTSD, and to this day she doesn't like to be in the dark. We have to sleep with a night light on in the room. But if it makes her feel more comfortable, I'll do whatever it takes.

After she told the police everything that happened, they were able to find the other cabin where Jace had kept her, and had enough evidence to prove he was killed in self-defense. She was finally free of him for good.

She finished her anti-hack program and sold it to an advanced tech company for just over eight million dollars. She has made two upgrades since then, and I was lucky enough to snag one for my company. She has taken over as supervisor of the cyber department and has everything running so smoothly, Reed has barely anything to do.

She comes strolling back inside and, as she walks past me, slides her hand across my chest before grabbing my tie. "Whata' ya' doin' handsome?" she purrs as she pulls me toward the downstairs laundry room.

I smirk and gladly follow. "Whatever you want baby," I tell her, because I would literally do anything for this woman. She and our kids are my entire universe. She glances around the corner to see the kids playing contentedly in the playroom, and then she closes and locks us in the laundry room. She immediately starts unbuttoning my dress shirt, and I loosen my tie.

Once my shirt is off, I lift her up by her butt and place her on the running washing machine. Her eyes widen as she feels the vibration under her, but they soften slightly in pleasure. I quickly hike up her dress before unzipping and freeing my rock-hard cock from my pants.

"You're so fucking sexy, you know that?" I smile against her lips as I kiss her. She moans as she wraps one hand around my back and the other into my hair. I rub the tip of my cock through her silky folds to coat myself in her juices before I line myself up to her entrance, and slowly slide home. "Fuck, baby. I love this pussy. Feels so goddamn good wrapped around my cock," I groan into her neck as I kiss and lick there.

She tilts her head back, using her hand on my hair to keep me there, and then she whispers in my ear, "Now fuck me with this big cock."

I moan as I grab her plump ass in both hands and thrust my hips forward till I've bottomed out inside her. She whimpers at the feel of me. "That's right, baby girl, daddy's going to give you what you need," I growl out as I continue to thrust my hips hard against hers, making sure to roll my hips at the end so they rub against her clit.

"Yes, daddy, more!" she moans.

Using one hand, I yank the front of her dress down to expose her full, round breasts. I pluck and flick at her nipple as I fuck her ruthlessly. The sound of slapping skin echoes in the small space. "So..." *thrust...* "Fucking..." *thrust...* "Wet..." *thrust.* I slide my hand that was playing with her gorgeous tits down to her clit before pinching it between my fingers.

"Ahhh..." she shouts, and I quickly kiss her to cover the sound as she falls apart for me. Her body clenches down on my cock like a vice. I fuck her through it to maximize her pleasure before she leans forward and whispers the magic words in my ear. "Fill me up, daddy."

My hands go back to her ass as I fuck her so hard, the washing machine slides across the tile floor. Three more thrusts, and I'm giving her just what she asked for—filling her tight little cunt with my cum. I drop my head to her shoulder and groan at the feeling.

Sex with Aleice continues to be amazing. Doesn't matter that she's been my wife for over four years now, the chemistry and passion we've always had is still there.

I pull out and grab a towel before cleaning her up. "I love you Ally, babe," I tell her as I help her down from the washer.

"I love you too, big daddy." She winks at me before righting her dress and going to check on the kids. I don't know how I could possibly love my wife anymore than I already do, but day after day, it somehow grows.

We still go up to my cabin for a week every Christmas with the kids. It's become our family tradition. It's paying homage to her mom and how they used to spend the holidays, and also to us and how we feel in love. The kids absolutely love it there.

I don't know what I did to deserve her, but I'm so grateful she's *mine*.

THE END

ACKNOWLEDGE-MENT

I want to thank my husband for listening to my crazy stories and supporting me.

I also want to thank Kamaryn with a K editing for all your help with editing my books and fixing all my numerous mistakes.

I wanted to thank the other authors on TikTok and Instagram that I have befriended and have been so helpful with providing information and tips to help me improve.

I couldn't have done it without your help. I can't say thank you enough.

I also want to take the time to thank the readers, without you my dreams wouldn't be coming true. Thank you so much and please continue to enjoy my books.

ABOUT THE AUTHOR

E.r. Hendricks

E.R. Hendricks Is originally from Connecticut but now lives in Missouri with her husband and kids. She is a hot mess mom to 5 kids and two fur babies. If she isn't reading books, she is writing  them. Her hobbies include reading, writing, eating, sleeping and listening to music. She is new to writing but truly loves it, she writes romance novels. Tropes very depending on the crazy characters inside her head. With a soft spot for admittedly a little psychotic men and bad ass women. You won't find any meek and frail women in her books. She hopes you will enjoy her books as much as she enjoyed writing them.

BOOKS BY THIS AUTHOR

Out Of The Shadows

Katerina is a funny, badass, ADHD having necro-mancer/vampire hybrid.
She's sassy with a bit of crazy.
and when she finds herself at not only a new school but an entirely new country, things are bound to go wrong.

Kiazer is a necromancer who is on the road to a successful position as Dean of Runsfield Acadamy and a committee member for the Supernatural community.
What happens when things aren't as they seem and his whole world changes?
Will he change with it and go against everything he knows for her?

Out of the Shadows is the first book in a stand-alone series with material that may be difficult for some readers. This book has a HEA. It is recommended for 18+ due to language, sexual situations and violence. If you like spicy this book is for you. Happy reading.

The Pitch

I'm in love with my best friend's brother.
Too bad the last time he saw me I was fourteen and a dork.
Oh, and did I mention he plays for Manchester United, lives in Europe and dates models?

After a rough time in high school, I'm ready to start fresh.
When the chance to study abroad presents itself, I can't turn it down.
With a chance to get away and be closer to Aiden I won't pass this up.

The odds are stacked against me and the risk of losing my lifelong best friend.

Will Aiden finally see me, or will I continue to be just his sister's nerdy best friend?

The Pitch has material that may be difficult for some readers, check trigger warnings. This book has a HEA. It is recommended for 18+ due to language and sexual situations. If you like a little dark with your HEA this book is for you. Happy reading.

In Too Deep

The Mountain has always been my safe place, until it wasn't.

It was the place I went to escape from my mundane 9-5 desk job. My secret spot that allowed me to finally take a deep breath and clear my head.

It's where I escaped the darkness that always follows me.

I never thought it would all come crashing down around me.

Trapped with nowhere to go, I am forced to depend on the one man I promised myself I would never even speak to again, none-the-less depend on.

In too Deep is a novella with enemies to lovers, forced proximity, CEO/boss, age gap tropes. This book has a HEA. It is recommended for 18+ due to language, sexual situations and violence. If you like spice this book is for you. Happy reading.

Out Of The Realm

Release date-TBD

I watch her from the shadows of the other realm.

She's become my deepest obsession.

I kill anyone who touches her

She is MINE, and I will not share.

I feel his energy when he's around

I feel his emptiness and his... urges.

But I'm up for a challenge, just like my plants, with a little bit of TLC they always come back.

I will save him from himself, or maybe he will drag me to the other realm with him.

Out of the Realm is the second book in The Runsfield Academy Series. With material that may be difficult for some readers. This book has a HEA. It is recommended for 18+ due to language, sexual situations and violence. Check TW! If you like spicy this book is for you. Happy reading.

The Book Witch

Release date-TBD

Have you ever wished you could spend time in

your favorite book?

Have you ever wanted to go on wild adventures with your favorite characters?

Maybe have a book boyfriend you wouldn't mind visiting?

Cassie was living every book nerds dream at her book shop where the books call to her.

One touch and a spell she can travel into any book she wants.

With a minute in the real world being a week within the book, she can have the best of both worlds.

Living in her apartment above the book shop, with her cat Binks (yes like Hocus Pocus) she is content to run her little shop and turn into an old bitty with a bunch of cats.

Determined to never fall in love after how her father left her mother.

Cassie prefers to live in the land of fiction, where there are happy endings.

But what happens when one of Cassie's adventures get a little too real and she falls for one of the characters within the book?

This book has a HEA. It is recommended for 18+ due to language, sexual situations and violence. Happy reading.

The Devil You Know

Release date-TBD

They say the devil is in the details, I'd say I'm in a lot more than that.

Running a billion-dollar company is hard enough but also making sure the sins are maintained is becoming...troublesome.

My business thrives on the sins of others, but when those pesky Angels step in and start influencing miracles and sinning goes down I'm forced to handle things myself.

I won't let those feathered fucks stop me from achieving my ultimate goal. I will have their sins and I will bask in the glory all the way to the top.

For I am the Devil and you must give the devil her due.

This book has a HEA. It is recommended for 18+ due to language, sexual situations, and violence. This book is on the darker side so be mindful if that isn't something you enjoy. Happy reading.

Fated Moon

Release date-TBD

This book is a why choose (brothers) wolf shifter romance.
Blurb to come.

His Savior, Her Obsession

Release date-TBD

This is a younger guy older girl, young adult dark romance. Blurb to come.

The Alpha's Captive

Release date-TBD

This is a syfy Alien romance.
Blurb to come.

This Is The End

Release date-TBD

This is a zombie/post-apocalyptic romance.
Blurb to come.

Printed in Great Britain
by Amazon